The Weaver's Loom

Eva held her tears as she watched her only son racing down the path, a tiny hand in Iza's grasp, his chubby legs trotting to keep pace. Iza bent down to say something to him. Eva could barely see the glimpse of a smile as they walked out of sight. She fought the overwhelming urge to collapse on the ground and sob, or chase him down the path, for she knew her interference would seal his fate.

She stood outside the cabin, watching the ghostly image of her son being led away, innocent to the shadow that obscured his future.

I've left his fate in the hands of another. Have I done the right thing, Lord? Have I failed my only son?

She prayed to God for His mercy, for His protection, for safe passage, gladly offering her own life in trade. Eva heard the crack of a gun in the distance and she broke for home. She ran through the trees, branches snapping against her body, and sobbed great, heaving sobs. The cacophony of automatic gunfire chased her, followed by a blaze of fire that licked upwards, beautiful against the emerging twilight stars.

What They Are saying About
The Weaver's Loom

The Weaver's Loom,

"Very intriguing and sensual writing. [The author's] inner poet certainly shines through. Great background development and storyline premise."

Dianne Helm, CEO
Helm Publishing

Wings

THE WEAVER'S LOOM

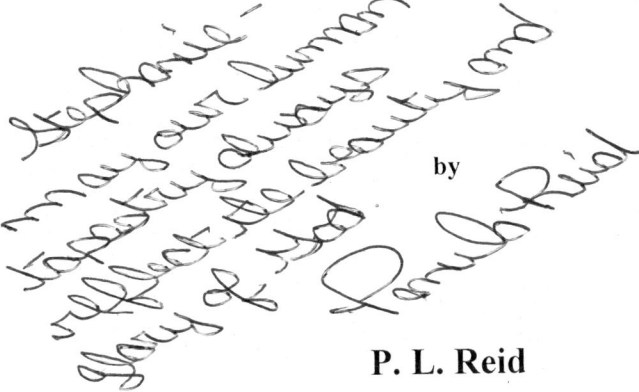

by

P. L. Reid

A Wings ePress, Inc.

Historical Novel

Wings ePress, Inc.

Edited by: Joan Afman
Copy Edited by: Joan Powell
Senior Editor: Pat Evans
Executive Editor: Marilyn Kapp
Cover Artist: Justin James

All rights reserved

Names, characters and incidents depicted in this book are products of the author's imagination or are used fictitiously. Any resemblance to actual events, locales, organizations, or persons, living or dead, is entirely coincidental and beyond the intent of the author or the publisher.

No part of this book may be reproduced or transmitted in any form or by any means, electronic or mechanical, including photocopying, recording, or by any information storage and retrieval system, without permission in writing from the publisher.

Wings ePress Books
http://www.wings-press.com

Copyright © 2010 by Pamela Reid
ISBN: 978-1-59705-524-6

Published In the United States Of America

October 2010

Wings ePress Inc.
403 Wallace Court
Richmond, KY 40475

Dedication

The character of Izabel Remény in *The Weaver's Loom* was sculpted from the indistinct oral history of a woman named Mary Lanka. Mary was also my great-great grandmother. Very little is known about her. We know that she was born on May 5, 1863 in a north Hungarian town in the Eastern foothills of the Bükk Mountains. We also know that Mary was a Catholic.

The single defining legacy Mary left to the world was two children fathered by a Jewish man in Miskoloz, Hungary. Oral history suggests Mary was ostracized for this transgression; however, we know for certain that she and her children emigrated from Hungary in the late 1800s, that she never married, and that she lived in Aurora, Illinois on Pigeon Hill until her death in 1930.

Historical accounts reveal Mary's life was not marked by grace and forgiveness, but rather, outright rejection by others in her community. Interestingly, my father was unaware of our Jewish heritage until my mother stumbled across this information while doing genealogy. This only served to amuse my father all the more, for he embodies decency, kindness and mercy in a way his forebears simply could not.

I am proud to dedicate this book to my great-great grandmother, Mary Lanka.

Before every man there lies a wide and pleasant road that seems right but ends in death.
(Proverbs 14:12 TLB)

One

Magdalena Szótemel scraped paint along a spiral staircase, moving slowly around a 100-year-old banister, when the stealthy movement of a spider caught her eye. She stopped to watch it melt into a crack in the floorboard beneath the secret window. She placed one finger over the crack and felt a draft on her skin. Sighing aloud, Magda pried loose the ancient floorboard, and there discovered her murdered father's letters.

She and her brother loved that secret window. With four burgundy stained-glass triangles nestled inside a small, round, wooden frame, it seemed, to a child's eyes, like a portal to another dimension. The red glass was quite filthy, for a person had to crawl along a narrow ledge on their hands and knees, and slide out over the top of the stairs, just to reach it.

At the bottom of the staircase sat an old radiator, hissing and sputtering and staring belligerently. Even if she managed to survive the fall, the cast-iron radiator would surely finish her off. Any child with the nerve to negotiate the ledge and crawl inside the nook would be completely hidden from prying eyes, for only those who followed could peek inside. So much greater, then, was the enjoyment of a long book in solitude.

Turning the letters over in her hand, Magdalena felt a terrible sense of foreboding. Before she untied the string, or strained to read the postmark, she sensed the terrible secret that had pressed itself onto her heart. She had an understanding that eclipsed knowing, like a person suffering a symptom with no knowledge of the disease.

This, however, was about to change.

Magdalena Szótemel turned her ear to the sound.

Drip, drip, drip, drop, drip, drip…

A gust of wind shook the water off the towering ash with its great branches reaching out over the sidewalk. Summers were brutal in the Midwest. The sun scorched the moist earth and the earth relented, giving up her damp, sinking, decaying organic matter, and released her precious water to the unforgiving sun.

Magda went out to her breezeway and watched a squirrel shake the rain from the lower branches of her flowering crabapple, as it sent tiny ping, ping, pings onto the neighbor's overturned trash can. She loved the smell of the earth after a mid-summer rain. She loved the red-breasted robins that came to her yard to gobble the earthworms that rose up from the mud. She loved the children who plucked them from the lake beneath her downspout, dropping them in a stinking mass inside little plastic pails.

She wished she were young again, splashing barefoot in the street, sun-burnt in her tank top and cutoff blue jean shorts, screaming wildly as she kicked water onto her brother's skinny legs. She turned her attention to the old cast iron basin sitting beneath her antique lilac. The raindrops fell into the reflecting pool, moving the water outward and then back again; shifting the ripples into waves.

Magdalena stared at the letters in her trembling hands and suddenly felt sick with fear, for she knew she had no choice but to unravel the mystery surrounding her parents, even if she unwittingly exposed the darkest moments of their lives as a result.

Two

Summer in Illinois. Aurora, Illinois. Aurora was the quintessential blue–collar town. To distant travelers she appeared slumped–over and exhausted from the vestiges of an early industrial era. She was a relic. She straddled the waters of her natural tributary, the Fox River, a fast–moving river nourished by the northern Chain O'Lakes. The Fox sustained many early pioneer settlements on its endeavor toward the shores of the Illinois River, and then on, again, toward the mighty Mississippi.

Not far from the bustle of midtown stood dozens of century-old Victorians. Elegant manors wore antique lilacs and European roses like colorful baubles along a graceful neckline. Massive granite urns, overflowing with snowy geraniums, crouched near stately walkways. Each gilded cage stood a respectful distance from the common passersby, behind wrought–iron lock and privy hedge, bearing silent testimony to the tremendous wealth that gave them life.

Spanning further outward along the eastern banks of The Fox were great pockets of immigrant settlers to the Midwest. Industrious, spirited, and resolute—these men and women were the bone and sinew of every newly industrialized prairie town across Illinois. Superior Street, Ohio, Beach Street, Root Street, Grove. Every block was a rural amalgam of Eastern European villages…a veritable United Nations. Every family was a single thread within a delicately woven tapestry—bright, colorful, and unique. Low–Germans, High–Germans, Hungarians and Romanians all converged together on Pigeon Hill.

Magda remembered walking the crowded streets of downtown Aurora as a girl, holding tightly to her mother's faded *háziruha*.

"Mrs. Patterman says that when she was little, Fox Indians would walk here to buy supplies. She says that she could actually smell them long before they even reached the town."

"Well…not smell them, exactly, but smell the skunk skins that they used to cover themselves." She wrinkled her nose as if faint remnants still lingered in the air.

"The Indian camp was along the river just south of here."

"What happened to the Indians, mama?"

"Oh, I don't know, csitri, they just went away, I guess."

Her mother seemed to offer this as an apology as she navigated her children past men slumped in doorways, music blaring from upstairs apartments, crying babies, the stench of urine. Magda moved alongside her, seeing the ghosts of dead Indians walking into town, their moccasin feet kicking up dust in the road as shopkeepers stared rudely from storefronts.

Pigeon Hill. This was her birthright.

Magda stood up from the kitchen table and padded barefoot across the Formica floor to an open window. She pulled a damp pile of kinky brown hair away from her neck and leaned against the screen mesh, flaring her nostrils, searching for a cooling breeze. There was none.

"Of course I remember that Gypsy witch," David said. "Every kid in the neighborhood was terrified of her! Remember when Jimmy Kyle climbed her east property wall on a dare? How he hit the ground screaming? Blood spurting from his hands and knees? Crazy Izzy laid broken bottles all along the top of her wall to keep the kids out of her yard. How could I forget about her, Maggie?"

Magda turned to watch her brother swirl beer around in his glass. He looked absently down at a slender hand. Wide-set brown eyes accentuated thick, sensuous lips. *Almost pretty...prettier than me,* she thought, as she wondered at the long lines of his nose and the soft blond curls framing his tanned forehead. David took another sip of his beer and shifted around in his chair.

"Hell, Maggie. I forgot how hot summer in Illinois can be."

"Wait right here," she said, and turned toward the stairwell before David had time to nod. At the top of the stairs she headed for her bedroom and, slamming the door shut, she stripped to bare skin in front of a full-length mirror.

She was Hungarian Jew. Her ethnicity slashed and burned its way across the landscape of her physique: tall frame, large-boned and muscular, short legs and a long torso, wide shoulders, hips and buttocks. Her grandmother's green eyes, too small for her face, were insignificant. It didn't bother her that she was ugly for she did have one lasting vanity—Gypsy hair. It was long, dark and wavy—so lustrous as to try and strangle an unwary hairbrush. She smiled at the defiant refusal of seduction by comb or gel or elastic band. It was strange to her that schoolyard torment would give way to her single, defining feminine guile.

She pulled a pink sundress up over her head and twisted her hair into a French knot. She secured the loose tresses with silver butterfly hairpins, snatched the letters off her nightstand, and pounded back down the spiral staircase to the kitchen below.

"I found some old letters and photographs I think you should see," she began.

"I'm tired, Magda, can't we just cut to the chase?"

"But..."

"Please, I haven't slept since I left New York. I am hungry and tired and I'm not up for all this melodrama. Please just tell me what the hell this is about."

"No, David, let the letters speak for themselves. Besides, I need your help translating the Hungarian dialect."

"Let the games begin," he breathed, pitching the letters across the table.

"Goddamnit, David, you're the family genius, why don't you read these letters and then you can explain them to me." She pushed the bundle back across the table. The twine came undone and letters spilled across his shoes.

"Though I'm sure you're barely able to comprehend..."

She interrupted his seething retort with a beeline back to her bedroom. This was their way–David's and hers. The trials Magda faced in adulthood were hauntingly familiar to those that tested her mettle as a child. *Fierce loyalties and rivalries spinning in delicate balance, and the bloodletting is not entirely without pleasure.*

David was the prodigal son. The family jewel. He was the single reason why her mother chose to live. And Magda was his rhetorical nursemaid.

She sat on the edge of her bed for several minutes to calm her nerves and then stormed back downstairs to the kitchen.

"David?"

"What?"

"Do you remember when you were five and I was eight and you set fire to a wastebasket in your bedroom? How, being the obvious influence for the disturbing behavior, I was forced to live in the basement for months, listening to Mama preen over you like a prized Yorkie."

"What are you talking about, Maggie?"

"If you appeared to be losing weight, it was because I ate your portion. When you smelled ripe, it was because I used all the hot water. If you swore at school, it was because you heard it from me. I learned to have eyes in the back of my head to steer clear of the back of our mother's hand."

Her mother didn't love her; she was sure of it. She merely tolerated her daughter's presence in exchange for upkeep of her fair–haired child. She did not remember a single instance when her mother spoke directly to her...about her. She did not remember her mother making eye contact or touching her or saying that she loved her.

One rare display of affection occurred as she sat on the floor at her mother's feet, leaning against her armchair, and her mother reached over and began to stroke her hair. She froze. She was afraid any movement would shake her out of her daze and send her away forever. They sat there for what seemed an eternity. She ran her fingers through Magda's hair and Magda trembled under her touch. Then it was over. She never touched her again. Magda was only ten years old.

"David, my agenda was shamelessly self-serving. If I cared for the person most cherished by our mother, I may someday earn her love in return. Or maybe a sparing portion would somehow leach onto me. I never outgrew this yearning, even after our mother's death, and this desire laid waste to a sizeable chunk of my adulthood."

"What exactly are you suggesting, Magdalena?"

"I don't think Mama was my real mother."

David regarded her coldly. "You need help, Magda."

The ensuing silence in the room was deafening.

"Have you lost your God-forsaken mind, Maggie?"

Magdalena belly-flopped onto a pile of pillows at the head of her bed and listened for the sound of footsteps on the wooden staircase. After a few minutes, she began pulling clips out of her hair and scratching the scalp underneath. She lay there scratching and listening for what seemed like an eternity before she finally rose softly and tiptoed to the bedroom door. She opened it a crack to listen for any sound from the kitchen below.

I know I didn't hear him leave. She reached for a sterling-handled hairbrush on the antique oak dresser. Suddenly, she heard David's chair scrape against the hardwood floor as he bent down to retrieve the spilled letters at his feet. For nearly two hours she lay in bed twirling her hair and listening to the rustling of paper as her brother sorted through their mother's faded letters. Again and again he returned to the refrigerator to refill his glass. The house was eerily quiet except for the sound of paper and breathing and the occasional gulp of beer. *Must be good news.* She drifted into a slumber, hair cascading over a mound of pillows.

What seemed like minutes later, she awoke to find David fumbling to tuck a large foot under her quilt. Though Magda knew he was drunk, she found the kind gesture strangely disturbing. His eyes were veiled in the dim light.

"I'm sorry, David."

"For God's sake, don't apologize," he mumbled. "Don't worry about it, Maggie, go to sleep."

"What did the letters say, David? Why did Izabel write mama all those years? Who was Shimon? And who was the baby mentioned in the letters from the village?"

"Ssshhh. Go back to sleep. We'll talk in the morning."

"Was she my real mother, David?" She held her breath waiting for the response.

"No."

She began to cry softly.

"What is real, anyway, Magda," he said sharply. Then, "What is real is that I love you, Maggie. I love you. Now go back to sleep. I'm drunk. We'll talk about it in the morning."

Great, she thought, *I've been rejected by two mothers. Could it get any better?* She lay in bed and cried until the sunbeams crowded around the edges of the window shade.

Three

He heard Maggie crying alone in her room upstairs as he dug around in his briefcase for a mescaline to go with the twelve-pack of imported lager he just drank. *At least she buys a decent brew.* He lay back on the couch pillows and waited for the drugs to kick in. He felt his body relax. His racing heart and pounding head slowed to a steady beat.

"I need a joint." He didn't bother searching the nooks and crannies of the old house since he knew Maggie never used. Magda medicated herself with different kinds of dope: food, wine, creeps, seclusion, work, and sleep. Lots of sleep. At least he slept off the customary hangover. Maggie slept because she knew she couldn't see her own reflection in her dreams. And she could see Mama.

He reflected that Mama was *un beauté classique*. Everyone loved her. She was petite, with long, slender fingers and toes. Her shoulder-length, wavy hair was the color of fresh honeycomb. A flawless butter-rum complexion was offset by dramatic red-brown lips. Mama's most dominant feature was her amber-colored eyes. Mama's eyes were filled with light. In the outdoor sunshine they were as reflective as the waves of a river. And in the lamplight they were silky and chocolate-brown.

David remembered Mama's closed-mouth smile that strangers thought was demure; only her children knew she hid a mouthful of crooked yellow teeth. *"Poor diet,"* she would say. Mama served fresh bread and whole milk at each meal. Breakfast, lunch and dinner. Every morning she rose at 4 a.m. and prepared the bread to rise. And every afternoon the trailing scent of fresh-baked bread beckoned them inside for a taste. Though his mother had been dead now for years, a sudden whiff of boiled cabbage or fresh bread still filled him with longing.

On Saturday afternoons, Mama dressed in her finest and walked her children into town. She smiled and waved at friends and neighbors on the street, stopping to chat along the way. Women admired her and men adored her. Though she was a young widow, the men maintained a respectful distance. A butterfly in a bell jar.

David smiled to himself at the memory. One day a young man—recently come to Aurora with the CB&Q Railroad—bounded up the walkway carrying a bouquet of fresh-cut flowers for mama. Mama smiled warmly behind her tiny hand and laughed happily at his mindless chatter, but she never once made a move to unlock the screened door. Neither charming compliments nor graceful invitations persuaded her to allow the intrepid suitor inside.

After many minutes the man turned to leave—his face and his feet dragging in defeat. He was met on the street by a small group of men. David stood up on his tiptoes at the door to hear the rise and fall of the voices outside.

"Come in from there," Mama said, closing the door behind her. They never saw the young man again.

He turned over and thought of his sister as a child. It wasn't surprising to him that Magda belonged to someone else. She was as plain as Mama was pretty. Magda ran the streets as a girl—unkempt and wild. Mama never touched her to clean her until the smell became a distraction and the schoolteachers complained. Magda's long hair would often be covered with dirt and leaves, and knotted into hard clumps. She tried to pick out the dried mud caked between her bare toes before coming inside for the night. She washed her hands and face fastidiously before each meal, forgetting the dust plastered in the creases of her neck and legs. Finally, when Mama had enough, she would shove Maggie into the tub and scrub her until she whimpered. Mama acted like touching her was like handling a poisonous snake.

Magda was great fun as a child. She was wildly imaginative and had an enviable sense of comedic timing. They spent long, summer days devising suspenseful plots and searing dialogue for their lavish theatrical productions. Maggie was always the starring actress. He felt privileged to be in her presence…swept away in her dreamscape. She and David were traveling companions in a world of their own making.

"I'll be Tom Sawyer and you'll be Huckleberry Finn, and we just uncovered a treasure-box inside a cave. There are empty powder-kegs, guns in leather cases, old moccasins, and a leather belt."

"What's a Huckleberry, Maggie?"
"It's a boy, silly! You're a Huckleberry."
"What do we do with the powder-keg?"
"That's what we use to load our guns."
"Why do we need guns?"
"To fight river pirates."
"Why?"
"They want to steal our gold coins."
"What gold coins?"
"The ones inside the treasure-box."
"Oh."
"Never mind. Let's play King Arthur instead."
They were best friends. Magda either didn't notice, or didn't care, about Mama's shameless neglect.

That was, of course, until their world opened to the ugliness of neighborhood gossip. The nuns at the St. Nicholas schoolyard were terrorists.

They would shake Magda, scolding, "You are a dirty little girl."

"No one loves girls who play in back–street alleys or climb tall trees."

"Nothing good will ever come of you."

"God will punish you."

"You will be taken away from your Mama."

David smiled as he remembered how they spent hours thinking up clever responses, such as cussing or spitting, or various other acts meant to shock the nuns to silence.

Most of the neighbors seemed sympathetic, but unwilling to get involved. Invitations to swim in a backyard pool usually led to the mom trying to wrestle a comb through Maggie's long, wet hair. Maggie would quickly lose interest in the hair-pulling session and run headlong down the block towards the High Street Bridge with her brother in hot pursuit. David grinned as he remembered how homemade dresses and skirts were often left on their front porch in large, plastic garbage bags. Magda threw them over her head and tore about the yard—impervious to the perils of running and jumping in a dress.

Tossing restlessly, David recalled that it had not taken long for her spirit to yield. By age eight, she was less animated and gregarious. This marked the beginning of Maggie's metamorphosis at the hands of her peers. Their cruelty was unprecedented...even for the hard–knock, east–side streets. The taunts of neighborhood boys were challenged with fists and teeth and hair. Magda was vicious in her attacks. Few boys on the block survived early childhood without a bloody lip or black eye courtesy of his sister. Even the hardened bullies learned to tease her from a distance, or in the vicinity of an adult, to discourage reprisals.

When David first started school, Magda not only tolerated her little brother's presence, she waited patiently for him at the teeter-totters at recess. It did not take him long to figure out why.

The girls were fiendish. They clustered together in packs.

"Hey, Jeannie! Look at my Malibu Barbie lunch box."

"Wow! That's really nice. My daddy bought me this gold locket."

"Really? My mother and I bought school clothes at Marshall Field's on Michigan Avenue."

David shuddered at the thought of the daily frenzy surrounding the latest trinket gifted the wealthier town daughters. Rich little girls flaunted their fashions while their friends hovered about to ogle. If Magda dared approach them, hungry second–string bitches, eager to climb the ranks of popularity, would move swiftly to close out the invader. If Magda persisted, whether out of pride or desperation, the girls cut her with their hateful descriptives of filthy Hungarian Jews.

"Excuse me, may we help you," they challenged.

"Your locket is so pretty, Jeannie. Can I see it?"

"Oh, sure, freak. And when you've smudged the gold case, my father can drive all the way back to Chicago to buy me a new one. God, you're stupid! Get your nasty–smelling butt away from here." The girls closed the circle with a fresh fit of laughter—eyeballs rolling in dismay.

Magda spent countless hours wandering the schoolyard alone after the stinging verbal assaults, carefully avoiding eye contact with her peers, but also refusing to return to the teeter-totters to play with David.

Magda learned to steer clear of anything that glittered, glowed or smelled sweetly. Blue jeans and tee shirts became her stock in trade. Magda had no girlfriends until she reached middle school. Fortunately for her, a student named Bibi Yeager from Louisville, Kentucky drifted into the spotlight formerly transfixed by David's infamous sister. Bibi's fully-developed body and shocking sexual behavior made her a perfect mark for the viciousness of pre–pubescent girls.

Bibi sometimes let David feel her up in their bathroom in exchange for marijuana cigarettes. God, he loved that girl. She was a sage; a visionary. A prophet with the sweetest tits east of the Mississippi. Apparently, her father thought so, too. The state police dragged him out of his house shortly after he arrived to Illinois. Though Mama regarded Bibi as white trash, her presence in their lives was tolerated, as it elevated their own social standing at the Ladies' Auxiliary luncheons.

Salmon. What the hell kind of color is salmon, anyway? Not exactly red, or orange, or yellow. Makes me want to throw up. Salmon is Maggie's favorite color. Figures. I'm surrounded by salmon pillows, throw rugs, blankets...

Reminds me of bloated road–kill on an August afternoon. Or rotting fruit. Or a sickening– sweet drink served in a plastic pineapple at the Holiday Inn. Lying here makes me feel I'm suffocating.

Funny. This is the way I always feel when I come home.

Four

Shimon never forgot the first time he saw her. She was just a wisp of a girl trailing behind her mother with a basketful of laundry balanced on one narrow hip. A field of yellow wood violets nodded its fervent approval of the Rromani folksong she sang to the trees and the sky. Gliding along the worn pathway to the river, she seemed entranced in some strange reverie.

The girl's mother clicked her tongue in disapproval of her daughter's idleness.

"*Siess!*"

The girl responded by setting down her basket to curtsy to the silver birch, oak, beech and chestnut. She then began a breathless spinning that sent her skirts flying up on her legs. The sight of her caught the air in the back of Shimon's throat and made his knees jerk uncontrollably.

The girl's blue dress was worn thin at the hem and wrists—the color faded from repeated scrubbings. Lavender blossoms were stitched along bare spots in the thinning material, and an embroidered sunburst of red, gold, green, black and purple rose up toward her tiny face. One wavy, black braid lingered against the center of her back and her skin was flawless and brown. Wide-set green eyes flashed in defiance at the back of her mother's plain red *diklo*.

Shimon sat against the trunk of an acacia, struck dumb at the sight of such exquisiteness. He felt a slight twinge of guilt at this unexpected voyeurism. He, himself, might have a child the same age, as he guessed her to be between twelve and thirteen years old. Beads of sweat gathered across his upper lip as he stabbed a leafy bookmark into place and called out to the pair.

"Hello, mama. Hello, *nyápic gyermek*." He spoke in Hungarian, as he leaned one arm against the trunk of his favorite tree.

Startled, the older woman whirled about to locate the strange voice. Her eyes narrowed as she searched his person, pausing at *yarmulke* and *kaffiyeh*. Her eyes then darted past him to find the location of her *čhej*. She called briskly to her daughter.

"Izabel! *Mangav ke aves manca*."

Shimon exhaled at the sound of the young girl's name and his eyes swept over her outline in the distance. Aware she was being watched, Izabel smoothed her crumpled dress and swept a few stray hairs off of her face. Every movement of her hands seemed deliberate, silky, with a feline grace. Green eyes locked his as she slowly bent at the waist to retrieve her basket of wash. He turned away quickly to avoid her open stare. His throat burned at the smooth outline of her tiny breasts heaving against the dress.

He smiled apologetically at the mother though he knew her sharp eyes hadn't missed his covetousness. The mother's rage boiled beneath her tongue as she spoke in icy servitude of his station.

"Sir, my name is Greta Remény and this is my daughter, Izabel. Pray you forgive our disturbance," she said, glancing down at his book.

"It is I who should apologize for having disturbed you, madam." Shimon bowed his head deeply. "I am simply taking a bit of solitude to read and reflect on the works of József Kürschak. I am Shimon Szótemel. I am a Halachist at the Temple Harzion in the next village."

Mama's eyes glazed at the introduction, though she managed a polite nod.

"My daughter and I are humble Rroma who know little of the teachings of great scholars and men of refinement such as you. We have heard of you, sir, and of your teachings at the Temple Harzion. We have also heard of your generous work with the Rromani camps across the border. You helped provide food and clothing to the children of our community on our journey from Romania to this desolate land. I ask God for the blessings of good health and prosperity on your entire family."

Though the eyes of the old woman were cast downward in deference, the sharpness of her words belied a deeper hostility. And mistrust.

Even now I am an outsider to these people, he thought. A flush of anger overcame his usual temperance.

Audacious woman! He felt the blood rush from his chest to his neck and cheeks and brow. He rose to his feet. His six-foot frame towered over the old woman. Instinctively, he tried to regain the advantage owed his class, gender and station.

"I am pleased to hear that my charitable endeavors are making a positive impact on communities such as yours. I feel that all persons of wealth and breeding are obligated to assist those...less fortunate souls...such as yourself and your daughter." He glanced casually past the mother to nod toward the girl. A defiant glare, identical to her mother's, suddenly transformed into a playful smile. Her eyes lowered shyly to gaze at the long, tapered fingers at the front of her dress.

Shimon's anger faded to a throb. Then, softer, "If your daughter is partial to literary readings, my wife and I have gatherings on the 1st and 3rd Sabbath eve of every month. We would love to have her join our group."

"How very kind of you, sir, but my daughter cannot read or write. She is my wash helper. We carry twenty baskets to the Tisza each week to earn a few coins for meat and flour. I have a house full of children to feed and a husband who travels great distances to find work. I could not spare her for one moment, sir."

"Madam, perhaps we could strike a fair bargain. Your daughter can do small loads of laundry in exchange for her schooling. My wife teaches many of the temple sons and daughters to write and read. She speaks Hungarian, English and Hebrew. She is not much older than your girl, and not a kinder person has walked the earth in my lifetime. Send her along to the temple next week and I will make the proper introductions, madam."

"I must decline, sir, it is an unfair trade. I think my Izabel too dull for learning. She takes after me in this way."

"But, madam, a few soiled shirts seem a pittance for the privilege of learning. Might you want such things for a child of your own blood? Heritage needn't be a burden for your children to bear; on the contrary, your daughter's heritage could distinguish her. Study may be her pathway to divinity. Did you not have such stirrings, yourself, when you were a child?"

"Pray no, sir, my thanks to you. Goodbye then."

Mama clapped her palms together and hastened toward the river. Her daughter slowly followed behind like a sullen child, her wicked eyes lingering over him as she sauntered past. He could not help but try to breathe her essence as she moved past him. Ashamed, he lowered himself to the ground like a dog and pretended to read, while a sly smile played about the corners of her red lips. He gathered his books and bolted towards the safety of home the minute she was out of his sight.

Five

"I met a young girl near the banks of the Tisza last week."

"Oh?"

"She was helping her mother with the wash. She is a Gypsy. Certainly the child is uneducated, but I sense great potential in her."

"I see."

"I want you to welcome her into our home, Eva. I want you to teach this Gypsy girl to read and write."

"What language?"

"English."

"English is a very difficult language to master, Shimon. It could take years for a Rroma, even one so young, to become functionally literate."

"I do not think so, wife. You have not yet seen the brightness in her eyes. Eyes of the rarest green. With a light shining deep inside."

"I see."

"God has called on each of us to help those less fortunate than ourselves. *And ye shall teach them your children, speaking of them when thou sittest in thine house, and when thou walkest by the way, when thou liest down, and when thou risest up.* Deuteronomy 11:19."

"She is a stranger to us. We do not know her people. It frightens me."

"Delivering a Gypsy from her own ignorance? Lifting her out of darkness and sin? Be sensible, Eva. This child will become a vessel for Him to fill according to His will."

"I don't know, Shimon."

"It is the right thing to do, Eva. I am your husband. Do you not trust me?"

"A formal education would certainly provide opportunities for her and her children."

"Yes."

"If God has moved your heart so, Shimon, I must trust you. You are my husband."

Their marriage had been arranged by a *Shadkhan* when she was a small girl. She remembered how she cried at the thought of binding herself to such an old man. They were married when Shimon was twenty-eight and she was thirteen. He was from an affluent family from the town of Siklós at the Hrvatskan border; made famous by a twelfth-century castle that stood on a plateau above the town. Siklós castle was ringed with thick walls and ramparts, concealing torture chambers and dungeons deep in its belly, and encircled by a wide, waterless moat. Her own village of Villány, a few miles east of Siklós, was at the center of a wine-growing region on the southern slopes of the Villány Mountains. Both towns rested in the rolling hills south of the Mecsek Mountain range and west of the river Danube.

The men of Shimon's family were men of great wealth—and of God. Her husband had studied throughout Western Europe and received his rabbinical tutelage from local scholars. Although many Siklós daughters fancied Shimon, tradition dictated he wed a girl from neighboring Villány. Eva was only nine when the *Shadkhan* arranged their first meeting at a Shabbat feast in Villány. She didn't know it was to be their first viewing by the parents and priests. A puffy and arrogant Shimon spent his time flirting with her large-breasted cousin, but Eva and her girlfriend were too busy dressing paper dolls to care. When her mother told her that she would be promised to him, Eva ripped the heads off all of her paper dolls and threw them in the mud. A nod and handshake with her father sealed the deal. Shimon breezed past as Eva wept against her mother's soft breasts. Their parents negotiated the terms of a dowry, set forth in a contractual *tenayim,* which was officially sealed by the breaking of a dinner plate.

Eva was introduced to the subtle art of seduction early-on. Skin, hair and clothing became issues of biblical importance. Food was prepared with her developing figure in mind. Daily baths were followed by a strengthening oil massage. Though she railed loudly against her metamorphosis into a pedigreed pig, her mother dismissed her outbursts with the wave of a hand...instantly reducing her to tears.

Shimon and Eva were reintroduced when she turned twelve. Their second meeting went better as, by then, she was intrigued by the status of their arrangement. Shimon's face, arms and chest had filled out and he'd grown a thick, black beard with streaks of silver running along his temples. He seemed more thoughtful and sincere, and she felt an overwhelming shyness in his presence. He smiled at her and extended his hand at the urging of the Rabbi, and she covered her mouth to hide her excitement. A year later, they were married.

~ * ~

When Shimon first mentioned the girl to Eva, she was struck dumb by what he was suggesting she do. She was familiar with the Rromani camps that migrated back and forth across the Romanian border. Rroma were a strange and secretive people. The men and the women were usually tiny and slender, with black hair, brown eyes and mahogany skin; corroborating the Yiddish proverb "the same sun that whitens the linen darkens the Gypsy." Many young men worked as migrant laborers for wealthy landowners. Her own family hired Rroma to repair leaking roofs, harvest crops, and tend sick animals. The older men forged cookware, horseshoes and farm implements that were peddled door-to-door by women and children. The women made baskets and brooms to be hawked alongside the metal goods.

It seemed to her family that Eva's grandmother relied on the Rromani craftsmen for her supply of primitive household items, but the real reason behind their visits to the camp was a fortuneteller named Madam Mina. After delivering food and clothes to "destitute" Rromani children, and a quick scout around the campsite, Nana glided nonchalantly towards the tent flap of the fortuneteller. Eva, skin vibrating with fear and anticipation, loved stepping through the darkened tent of

Madam Mina, tinkling brass bells announcing their arrival. Madam Mina turned from her work, clasped her jeweled hands together, and "bless God" for their safe return. Eva was never certain what place God had among the things hidden in the shadows of that tent.

There were amulets of sacred wood, bloodstones, mother-of-pearl, jade and crystals. Leathers and furs were tossed unceremoniously about the dwelling. Ominous jelly jars filled with strange liquids were assembled along primitive tables near the cook stove. Some of the jars contained the unborn fetuses of animals, misshapen and grotesque, staring vacantly at her from behind milky glass. The fortuneteller kept a pile of bird feathers in a basket on her healing table: peacock, seagull, magpie, pheasant, blackbird, nightingale, mallard, and dozens more she didn't know. The flight feather of a snow owl was kept in a glass jar to avoid some weird contamination.

Also on the healing table were root bitters that singed her nostrils from inside their paper boxes. Such medicinal herbs cured fevers, depression, arthritis, headache, menstrual cramps, and impotence and were prescribed to people for miles around. Mina treated anyone that came to see her, whether or not they could afford to pay.

Mina greeted them warmly though she seemed careful to avoid physical contact. Her thick mane had been brushed carefully back into one long braid, then cleverly wrapped around the entire circumference of her slender face. Antique gold hairpins and crystal beads poked out between the shiny rows of delicate braiding. Her face was an elegant caramel complexion, her lips a striking coffee brown. She always asked if they were hungry as her long skirts swept a wide circle across the dirt floor.

"*Lośeno sim te dikhav Tut! Te bešes tele.*" She motioned Eva to join her over a steaming kettle of *Sármi*, savory stuffed-cabbages flavored with spicy red peppers, or *Morenas*, a rich lamb stew. Then they would serve Nana a *Rromano Čajo*. This was brick tea boiled in a samovar and served in glasses filled halfway with mashed apricots. Madam Mina and she giggled as they held a sugar cube between their teeth while they drank, but Nana preferred to add the sugar to her glass instead.

None of this mattered anymore for Eva's lack of moral courage. She sat frozen in awkward silence when she heard the insidious rumors spread by her neighbors about the local Rromani population.

"Rebekah told me a band of Gypsies were stealing children to sell on the black market."

"How awful, Deborah. Have you heard about the seduction of local Jewish boys in the nearby woods and meadows?"

Once, when Eva was a young girl, she overheard Madam Mina and her friends whispering that Rroma were widely regarded as a primitive people that lied, stole, lived in filth and devoured anything they could kill. Bearing witness to such hateful gossip made her feel dirty—and ashamed. Eva knew in her heart the exploitation of such racial stereotypes and ethnic misrepresentation showed a staggering ignorance of Rromani culture and behavior.

It was common knowledge, even for a child her age, any association with the occult, real or perceived, could have stained the reputations of devout Jewish women like

Nana. Every wife knew precisely when her neighbor was on a "charity mission" to the camp, and conveniently arranged her own rendezvous accordingly. It was a sisterhood of conspiracy. Each woman knew of the certain shame that would visit her husband if the truth were revealed, and each worked to avert public exposure cooperatively.

~ * ~

Eva stared at the Gypsy. Izabel was a phenomenal beauty—perfect in face and form. Her limbs were long and muscular—her body already hardened with work—and her black hair glinted red and gold in the sun. She approached Eva's yard slowly, lagging behind Shimon. Eva saw she was just a child and she felt ashamed for her envy.

She stepped through the doorway of her kitchen with a dishtowel slung over her shoulder, brushed the loose strands of hair behind her ears, and raised her hand in greeting. Shimon raised his palm in return, straightening as he approached.

"Good day, wife."

He was a fine-looking man. Eva allowed herself a luxurious sweep across his tall frame before they entered the yard. The sight of his broad shoulders and long gait made her flush with pride. She never felt safer than when Shimon was near. He was her strength. Her heart and soul.

Eva waited patiently for them on the kitchen steps. Shimon strode up easily and kissed her full on the lips. Izabel, surveying her fingernails, raised her head and smiled. She had remarkable wide-set green eyes. She looked cat-like as she licked her lips and preened the shiny black curls that outlined her face. Eva felt a twinge of jealousy as the girl waited submissively for Shimon's direction.

"Eva, I'd like to introduce you to Izabel. Izabel is from the Rromani encampment west along the river. I ran into Izabel today on my way into town."

"How do you do," Eva murmured. She smiled and extended her tiny hand and Eva felt the hairs on the back of her neck stand up.

"*Tu san katji šukar!*"

"Izabel will be attending our weekly poetry readings, Eva. I would also like you to work with Izabel to teach her to read and write."

"I am so very pleased to meet you," Eva said. "I am sure that we will soon become great friends. Tell me, Izabel, what would you most like to learn from us here?"

"English."

"My sweet girl, English it is, then," said Shimon. "English and friendship." Shimon's face broke into an unabashed grin and he wrapped his great arms around them both in a hug.

"Wonderful. My two beautiful girls. Most wonderful."

For the first time since their introduction, Eva saw a genuine smile of happiness creep across Izabel's tiny face as she disappeared beneath Shimon's loving embrace.

Six

Izabel removed the hairpins that held the upsweep and unwound the coils to form a chestnut mane. Eva sighed and relaxed as Iza's fingers pulled through the soft tresses. Izabel felt a lump on her scalp and, sensing vulnerability, felt a murderous impulse. She could snap her neck in an instant. She could run a knife along her underbelly. Izabel sometimes had such thoughts—fleeting, thrilling, and unbearably thick. Like the liquid burn of opium billowing through the veins of an addict, she often yearned to fall headlong into the abyss.

Izabel loved her. She loved her so much she wanted to crawl inside her skin. She wanted to feel her breath around her like a blanket. Her hand paused at Eva's temple to feel her pulse—slow and steady—before she reached for the hairbrush. She brushed the hair in small sections, slowly gathering it into a single, shiny mass. She unscrewed the cap from her bottle of oil and poured a puddle into her palm. She rubbed her hands together until the warmth oozed between her knuckles. She applied an even coating onto the golden shafts of hair, pulling the oil through in long, even strokes.

Izabel used a wide-toothed comb to gather the hair to be braided. She decided she would give Eva a simple, three-sectioned braid instead of the French braid her husband preferred. She gently pulled her head backwards as she tugged on each section, catching a glimpse of the vein pulsating in Eva's neck. When she finished, Izabel wrapped her head tightly in a bath towel.

"The warmth will heat the oil and the hair will absorb it," she said.

Eva sighed and lifted herself off the floor to take her place on the bed.

"You know, Izabel, your English has really improved these past months. How long have you been coming here?"

"Six months."

"Has it been that long already?" Eva turned to look down at her on the bed.

"Yes."

"My Lord, it has then," Eva murmured. "We must begin planning a celebration soon. You've learned so much, your parents will be proud, Iza."

She placed her hands on her hips and looked at Izabel with an all-encompassing smile. Izabel felt herself shrinking beneath Eva's gaze. She was certain Eva would discover her terrible secret. She folded her arms nervously across her chest. Eva laughed aloud and began to tease.

"Don't cover them, Izabel; they will soon be the envy of the camp. All the other girls will cry at night because they were not blessed as you. You have a beautiful figure. Carry yourself proudly, my dear." She bent down to kiss her forehead.

"Thank you, sister."

"We *are* sisters, Izabel," she said with tears in her eyes. "I prayed to God for a sister when I was a child. God has finally answered my prayers, Izabel, all of them, for I have a secret to share. Shimon has said it is time we have a child together. I have been waiting so long to hear him say those words to me, Iza. I am truly blessed."

Izabel felt her heart split wide.

"Don't cry, Izabel, this won't change anything between us. You are my sister and you will help me prepare for this baby. I haven't spoken of this to anyone. We have so much to do to prepare for her arrival and you must help me. I cannot do this without you. There is no other person I can share my joy with, Iza, please don't be sad. Now let me arrange your hair as you like."

Izabel slid onto the floor with a thud and began to sob loudly.

"Hush, sister. We will always be together." She spoke in a whisper as she began to unbraid Izabel's long black hair into a sea of waves that flowed along the floor and under the bed. "I know of your loneliness. I know of your father. I know about these things, for I have heard Shimon speak of them. This is why I have asked God to give me a daughter that we could both share. A baby will help mend your broken heart, little sister, I know it will."

Eva glided her long, tapered fingers through her waist-length hair, pulling the tangles gently before picking up the hairbrush. "Soon you will be helping me braid my own daughter's hair, Iza," she said.

Izabel felt faint at the abomination that lay inside her belly, for she was in her second month of pregnancy with a child that shouldn't be hers. She didn't care. She rocked herself. She silently cursed Eva barren. *Wicked whore!* Eva knew about her baby, Izabel was sure of it, and now Eva would yoke Shimon to the marriage forever.

It wasn't fair. Shimon had pursued her relentlessly. When momma and she went to the river, Shimon waited beside the pathway, hidden in the tall grasses and overhanging tree limbs. Sometimes she saw him, other times she saw only the gifts he left her: Fresh cuttings of sweet heather; a downy nest filled with brown-speckled eggs; a tortoiseshell comb in the hollow of a mossy tree-limb. But her favorite discovery was a gold bracelet adorned with tinkling silver bells, cleverly poured into a hollowed-out goose egg. Izabel squealed at the sight of it and her mother rushed over to see.

"What have you found there, daughter?"

"Look, mama, an empty goose egg in the grass," Izabel said. With a casual gesture, Izabel dropped the bracelet into her shoe.

"Yes, it is a goose egg," she replied suspiciously.

"May I keep it, Mama?"

"No, Izabel, we must not bring this thing into our home. The unborn is missing from inside. It cannot be a good omen, daughter. Drop it to the ground this instant."

"But mama," she protested.

Mama knocked the egg out of her hand, smashing it onto the path, and raised her hand to strike Izabel. A movement in the tall grass startled her and she turned to peer into the overgrown field.

"Get on, daughter, we have work to do this morning."

Izabel knew Shimon watched her, but she was never afraid. She delighted in the power to hold his eyes for she knew in her heart that he was afraid. She pranced behind Mama, swinging her hips. She ran her hands along her breasts and played with the curls against her face. The pathetic man panting in the shadows could not ignore her.

When Izabel was a tiny girl, she stumbled upon a wealthy town daughter lying on her back in the choking weeds, making love with a boy Izabel didn't know. As the boy greedily suckled the girl's breasts, her nipples rose to sharp points. She let him fumble between her legs with his seeking fingers, and then demanded he remove his trousers so she could explore him. The boy was veined and throbbing and the tip of his manhood glistened. Izabel watched as the girl gently touched the quivering mass that hung below, daring to taste the clear liquid that oozed from the top. Moaning, he pushed her head down, shoving the entire thing into her mouth. She gagged and threw up.

The girl cursed her lover while he pulled up his trousers to escape. Izabel suddenly heard the sound of other boys' laughter a few yards away. She also heard the sound of men rising from tents to inspect the disturbance. The boy shoved the girl to the ground and covered her face with one dirty hand. "Shut up, you filthy little bitch," he snarled. "You tell anyone about this and I'll give it to you good." He slammed the girl's head backwards onto the ground and tore out of the brush. Izabel ran home, terrified.

On a late summer afternoon, only four months after meeting her beloved Eva, Izabel's mother fell ill, and her father could not stay home to care for her. Izabel was assigned the washing chores. Her favorite brother George was sent to chaperone, but Izabel tempted him with an afternoon of fishing, and they split up a mile down the road. As she walked past a familiar strand of trees, she fanned her thighs with raised skirts to cool her from the heat. It seemed eerily quiet. She tugged at her blouse to cover herself as she quickened her steps. Suddenly, she lifted her skirts to run. She was in the air—her face covered. When she tried to call to her brother, she choked on the taste of cotton. And dust. She lay flat on her back and looked up at two, bright eyes.

"Did you like my gifts, Izabel?"

"Go to hell," she spat in her native tongue.

"You didn't like my gifts, then, little one?"

"I beg you to let me go." She spoke in Hungarian. She struggled against his pressing weight.

"I have wanted to touch you for so long. I feel drunk with you. I am afraid I can't control myself."

He placed his mouth against the skin at the base of her neck and breathed in a rasping breath. He continued down to the rise of her breasts beneath her dress. She gasped when she felt his lips brush her bare skin.

"How beautiful you are, my darling! Oh, how beautiful."

She tore at the short hairs along Shimon's ears and he gently placed his hands over hers—biting down into the soft tissue of one breast. She cried out in pain and turned her face away.

"No, Shimon!"

"Like a lily among thorns is my darling among the maidens."

"Please, I beg you!"

"Arise, my darling, my beautiful one, and come with me."

"I beg you not to do this!"

"Do not arouse or awaken love until it so desires."

"Stop it! Please."

Shimon rolled the top of her dress down to expose her breasts and raised her stomach to his mouth.

"Your navel is a rounded goblet that never lacks blended wine."

"Do not do this, Shimon, or I swear I will die!"

Lifting her skirts in one fluid motion, his hand glided along the inside of one thigh.

"Open to me, my sister, my darling, my dove, my flawless one."

She moaned as he explored her, her hips rising to meet him. When he opened her legs, she begged him to stop.

"Please!"

"You have stolen my heart, my sister, my bride; you have stolen my heart with one glance of your eyes, with one jewel of your necklace."

Why are you doing this to me?"

She twisted her body, but he maneuvered between her.

My God. No!

She rode the wave of pain when he entered her, and she wept when he cried out in release.

"I will never let you go, Izabel."

He couldn't. Not now. She wouldn't let him. He was the father of her child. His marriage could no longer be binding. He was a man of God, a good man, an honorable man. This was why she chose him, wasn't it?

Secretly, Izabel despaired the loss of her virginity. For the Rromani people, virginity was a requirement at the time of a first marriage. If it were discovered Izabel had been deflowered outside her bridal bed, any subsequent marriage would be instantly annulled. Worse yet, if her humiliated husband decided to pursue charges against her of *Daravipe,* accusing her of marital infidelity, he could demand a penalty—even her physical disfigurement. The pathway to her future was set, and she had chosen the path of her heart.

All this she conspired as Eva put the finishing touches on the elegant French twist.

"You are the most breathtaking woman I've ever seen."

Izabel looked into the hand mirror Eva offered, but it wasn't her own reflection she gazed upon. She studied the face of the friend who peered over her shoulder, admiring her handiwork.

"Not as blessed as you."

Seven

Sarai Indulat told her daughter not to befriend that Gypsy. She didn't understand why Eva was so sentimental about Izabel. The girls had nothing in common—no history to share. She even wondered why everyone thought Izabel so comely; frankly, she thought the girl had the refinement of a troll.

It was her overbearing pride Sarai found most-chafing. Izabel floated about her daughter's home like the fairest butterfly ever to grace the Plaines of the *Alföld*. Her hands itched to strike her when Izabel glared up from the parlor floor, legs spread out before her, books strewn haphazardly about. Sarai commonly referred to Izabel as 'the stain on the upholstery.' Why did she bother to teach such an illiterate? Besides, how could a female put such knowledge to good use?

"Born into a den of thieves."

"Oh, Mama."

"Don't you roll your eyes at me, girl, I'm not playing with you. You don't know what you've brought into your own home. Don't come crying to your father and me when your silver goes missing."

Sigh.

"And what of your husband, Eva? How can you properly tend to him with that lizard creeping about? A husband must have hot meals and clean clothes and time with his wife." She added a special emphasis on the last.

Eva continued sewing.

Her daughter was like the clear, white light of morning. She was young—not yet twenty-one. Eva believed she was doing good works in the eyes of the Lord. However, the Jews of Hungary have had a long history of repression and violence done to them in His blessed name.

The first expulsion of Hungarian Jews occurred in 1349 when they were accused of spreading The Black Death throughout Eastern Europe; so began many such assertions by non-Jews against her people.

Two centuries before the plague marched across the continent, the Church began its malevolent influence into the affairs of Jews. At the council of *Szabölcs*, Church leadership forbade intermarriage between Christians and Jews, and prohibited Jewish ownership of slaves. Funny how the Church was somehow able to intertwine the principals of marriage and slavery. She smiled at that. Though she strongly opposed the idea of intermarriage, Sarai found any law forbidding such practice morally reprehensible.

In 1279 Hungarian Jews were compelled to wear a "Jewish badge" and forbidden ownership of Hungarian land. The desire to mark the Jews was again revived in recent years by the Nazi Party. Nazi lack of originality was surpassed only by their strength of conviction and their penchant for brutality.

It isn't enough they bleed us for the murder of their Christ, she thought. *They need to brand us for organized disposal.*

And so the bleeding continued. At the 1494 blood libel in Tyrnau, sixteen Jews were burned at the stake. Another blood libel in the Hapsburg dominion of Hungary resulted in the burning of thirty Jews at the stake. The "Jewish Oath" and Jewish marriage permits added more kindling to the flames of hatred for Hungary's Jews.

The fires cooled when in the 1860's, Jewish citizens were suddenly afforded civil liberties not seen in recent history. With the freedom to pursue livelihoods and settle freely, gentiles could do little to stem the tide of Jewish businessmen, merchants, scholars, lawyers and doctors into lives of wealth and privilege.

Anti-Semitism metastasized into political ideology in the 1870's. This transition in thinking gave birth to the most systematic violence seen by Jews in recent history. Material wealth was increasing at a time when entire classes were laid waste by the new capitalist economy. Covetousness and fear fed the wellspring of hatred for Jewish wealth. Jews were depicted as human parasites feeding on the masses. The response by the Magyar people was another blood libel in Tiszaeszlor in 1882.

Jewish complacency deepened when in 1895 the Jewish religion was officially recognized by the state, an equanimity that afforded them equal rights with Catholics and Protestants. This recognition came to pass despite rigorous objections from the Church and its allies, who managed to delay ratification on three separate occasions.

And how did their Jewish brothers respond? With arguments and apologies! They brainlessly believed the emphatic denials of Magyar politicians and so failed to initiate any organized action. This anemic response by Jewish leadership would cost them millions of lives within a single generation.

The Catholic People's Party continued rallying against "anti-Christian" and "destructive" ideas, which, they asserted, were integrally linked to Jewish ideals. Liberals and socialists were the enemy; it was a short leap to include Jewish evildoers in the fight for the divine soul of Hungary.

The Jews continued to align themselves with Hungary even while their own scholars and clerics were targeted for attack. Other minorities felt little sympathy for Jewish violence as they viewed them as conspirators with the government.

Nineteenth-century Jewish culture was splintered between the conservative Orthodoxy and those advocating modern culture and assimilation. The liberals became known as Neologists and their calls for integration further served to widen the gulf between Hungarian Jews—weakening their resolve to defend their neighbor against attack. The chess pieces were dangerously aligned and the survival of the Jewish people was balanced along the blade of a knife.

Under the Orthodox leadership of Moses Sofer, Torah study became widespread throughout Hungary and *Yeshivot* were established in every community. Out of this conservative movement came Hungarian rabbinate and *Halakhists* of the highest standard. Many great authors of religious works and renowned community leaders were born during this time of great courage.

Although Eva had been born into privileged society, her bloodline was strengthened by her union with the

Talmudic scholar from Siklós. It should be no surprise the street urchin would desire to be in her company. But, as Sarai's grandmother used to say, "Never wear your finest satin outside in the rain."

On her last visit, Sarai saw the Gypsy huddled against the stovepipe, legs drawn up against her chest, an open notebook balanced on one skinny knee. There was a flush in her cheeks Sarai hadn't noticed before. She was quiet and withdrawn. Sarai tried to draw her into a conversation but the girl only responded quietly with hardly a sideways glance.

Sarai wasn't a monster. At times she pitied the girl. God only knew what squalid conditions she lived in at home. Izabel's father was not a Rrom, but a shiftless field hand who, once having secured the trust of Iza's family, snuck off to marry one of their beloved daughters. As a result of her defiance, Izabel's mother was forced to live outside the Rromani encampment while her husband left to find work. While the Rroma loved Izabel's mother and her children, they only tolerated the *gadžo's* presence in order to keep a watchful eye over his wayward family.

Izabel's father was an uneducated drunk who openly reveled in the company of whores. While his face was handsome and refined, his smile was tauntingly cruel. Izabel's father was reviled by Rroma and *gadže* alike, and so took his frustrations out on his Rromani wife, oftentimes with shocking violence. Once, he publicly beat her in the face with the heel of his boot.

Sarai remembered seeing him at market many years earlier. A woman didn't require a translator to understand the foulness he spoke to Izabel's mother. It was his eyes that told the true meaning of his words to her heart. The wife seemed frozen. When a passerby shamed him from the street, he began to curse, and smack her on the head like a sullen mule. As he dragged her down the street by her shawl, their children trailed just beyond the blast zone. The little ones cried for their mama while the older children tried vainly to blend into the crowd.

It was then that Sarai remembered first seeing Izabel. A frail child with enormous green eyes, she sobbed hysterically and held up her arms for her mother. When the father heard her noise he spun around. He swept her up into his arms, kissing the hair on her wet cheeks, as he staggered towards camp. Not even the noisy street could erase that sound from Sarai's ears. The girl's cries haunted her for days.

Izabel's mother and brothers continued past a group of village boys. Without a man present, the juveniles spat on the ground and filled the air with catcalls as she passed. Izabel's mother looked as exhausted as Sarai had ever seen any woman before or since.

Sarai didn't know what wickedness the father had done to his only daughter. However, she did know it was no child that sat at her feet this day. She studied Izabel for the telltale signs—swelling about the hands and feet, breasts swollen heavy with milk—but her flowing skirts and woolen shawl kept her secret.

Now was not the time for her daughter's family to draw attention. These were black days for their people and outsiders must be approached with caution. True, the Gypsies were only a ragtag band of beggars and thieves. Still Sarai feared to be in their midst. They often played music for *fillér* on the streets, but she never missed the opportunistic glint when a pretty girl passed, or when some fool opened his wallet nearby.

They were a few shades lighter than the tribesmen of Africa, with equally unsavory physical characteristics. To her eyes, they seemed a strange racial mix—a genetic cocktail so exotic as to be indefinable. She especially pitied the children to be raised so far from the grace of God. They could use a generous dose of the Lord's spirit...with perhaps a good scrubbing to help it stick.

They wandered the streets like desert nomads. They had no home, no culture, no written language—no identity. That was fine with her, let them stay invisible, she had her own to tend to. Eva was in her first weeks of conception with her first grandchild. Though tradition held out hope for a namesake—she secretly wished for a girl. A beautiful girl that would take afternoon tea while chattering on about schoolwork and boys.

According to an ancient Midrash, God forces a soul to enter a new being at conception. The soul is reluctant to relinquish its freedom for a stay on earth. But it has no choice. In the mother's womb, a light burns over the new child's head that lets it see from one end of the earth to the other. The child has complete knowledge of the Torah and of life and death. But just before the child is born, she is touched by an angel, causing her to forget this infinite wisdom. Folklore tells that the indentation on the upper lip is the permanent mark of the angel's touch.

Yes, in her heart, she wished for a girl.

Eight

Magda sat on the arm of the couch and pretended not to watch the clock tick the minutes past the hour. Hollow laughter bounced off the back walls of the room. It was easy to blank-out when mindless chatter belched out of a cheesy black box. She picked up the remote and began flipping through stations.

Dammit, he's late again, she thought.

Why do I set myself up for disappointment? I'm an idiot.

She was a thirty-year-old woman, but when he stood her up, she felt like she was fourteen again. Not that she was ever stood up in high school. You'd have to be asked out on a date first.

Why am I sitting here waiting on him again? I can do this myself.

Magda clicked off the television to go wash her face. She was careful not to look too long in the bathroom mirror. She dried her hands and went to write a note in case Paul decided to show. Magda taped the paper to a round, glass insert in the front door—muttering *"asshole"* under her breath.

Only last week, on her 30th birthday, she'd waited for more than two hours for Mr. Wrong to pick her up for dinner. Finally, she called his married friends in the city, to make sure he was alright. Or, that's what she told herself, at any rate.

"He's playing tennis with Phillip. I think they're going out for some guy-time afterwards."

"He was supposed to be here at four o'clock to pick me up for dinner. It's my birthday."

"Well, like I said already, he isn't here. How did you get this number, anyway?"

She heard later that the wife thought she was a pretty sad case; calling around to find a man that had stood her up on her birthday.

"She can't have much self-esteem to be willing to deal with that. If a man ever did that to me, I would change my number before I called around looking for him!"

When Paul casually mentioned his friend's reaction later that night, Magda's anger switched to defensiveness.

"I guess she wouldn't know what she'd do, since it was her husband you were hanging out with."

Then to bitterness.

"Sanctimonious bitch!"

Then despair.

"I haven't even had a chance to make a good impression on them yet."

In the end, she apologized for her mistrust, her immaturity and, most-importantly, for having embarrassed him in front of his friends. Every time this happened, Magda felt more confused, and humiliated, than the time before.

Paul's sexual gymnastics were impressive. But his secret weapon was his uncanny ability to shift blame. He made a fantastic victim. Throughout the course of their relationship,

Magda's feelings for him seesawed between awe and disgust. No matter, she didn't have anything better going these days; after all she was thirty, not exactly at her peak of freshness. Besides, she wasn't ready to forfeit the pleasures of sex yet.

For weeks she'd begged for intimacy, but he argued he was too tired, or had to be up early. *Must be getting some on the side*, she thought. She never allowed herself to dwell on such truths for very long. She'd barely be able to function if she did.

Magda shook herself out of her reverie, threw on a jacket and muffler, and grabbed the keys off the kitchen table. The storm door slammed behind her as she headed for her car. She placed the bundle of letters on the seat beside her and headed across town.

Mrs. Hencz used to live in the two-story, white clapboard across the street on Superior, but her children moved her across the river when the neighborhood started to turn. Magda remembered her as the tiny Hungarian lady who spoke broken English; who made mouth-watering caramel apples for her and David every Halloween. It was one of the few comforts she remembered as a child.

The old woman's face was deeply wrinkled from a lifetime of hardship and an affinity for unfiltered tobacco. She'd always made a fuss over Magda as a teenager, never drawing attention to her oily hair and bad complexion. If God had given Madga the choice, she would have asked to be Mrs. Hencz's little girl.

The retirement community was nothing fancy. Postage-stamp-sized yards were mowed by landscapers while tenants fussed in carports and flower borders. Not a blade of grass looked out of place. Hedges were trimmed and tidy, trees swayed across clean-swept sidewalks.

Magda loved old people. They always took time to listen. The old men reminded Magda of fussy, flapping hens. She watched them tiptoe gingerly down the block, holding onto their wife's elbow for support. They congregated at local barbershops to gossip and complain. Magda wondered if the virility God stole from the elderly was replaced with a refinement never realized in their youth. A refinement of spirit, distilled into a single human life, to be looked on with wonderment.

The women seemed tougher—resolute. Translucent skin, blue veins and thinning hair did nothing to dilute the strength of their voices. Magda wondered what Mama might have looked like if she'd lived so long. She was glad that she didn't. She would always remember Mama young.

Magda pulled her car up onto the curb in front of Mrs. Hencz's house. It had pale-yellow siding and red window boxes overflowing with petunias. A tiny welcome sign swung in the wind—banging against the porch frame.

Magda sidestepped the vehicle and pulled open the mailbox. The front door swung open, right on cue, and Mrs. Hencz waved at her like a child as Magda made her way towards the house.

"*Av Akai*, Magdalena!"

Magda noticed parted sheers falling back into place next door. She imagined the phone calls circling about them in the lines overhead.

She cleaned her shoes on the doormat and entered the home. There were delicate, lace curtains hanging in the front windows. An orange tabby sat blinking on a threadbare easy-chair. Knickknacks were scattered along the length of a buffet table and an antique hutch was bursting with blue china plates.

Everything in the house felt out-of-proportion. Magda guessed it was because of the downsizing after her husband's death. Her home was impeccably clean, dust-free, except for a lingering odor of moth crystals wafting up from the sofa cushions.

"Come in, come in."

She gestured towards the kitchen at the back of the house. The living room is kept for company, but the kitchen is the heart of the home; this is where the women gathered to reveal themselves.

Magda noticed the kid-art lovingly displayed on the refrigerator door and politely inquired about her grandchildren.

"Oh, my dear, they are such a handful. I don't know where they get their energy. I wish I could bottle it. I'd be a rich woman."

"Mrs. Hencz, I wondered if you could tell me about my mother."

"Oh, darling, we all loved your mother. She was a virtuous woman.

"No, Auntie, I mean my *real* mother."

She paused a moment as Magda sprang the trap.

"I don't know what you mean."

She looked down at papery hands. Madga gently said, "Mrs. Hencz, I found a bundle of letters hidden inside my mother's house. Can we please talk about it?"

"Oh, darling, I know very little about how you came to be in Eva's care. I can only say that you were blessed, indeed, to have had such a dedicated mother."

Magda knew the old woman would never tell her mother's secrets, so she asked her to translate a few letters instead. She hoped that the old lady would mistakenly give insight into their meaning. David helped with the basic translation, but there was still much she didn't understand.

"Times were different then, Maggie. People who came from small villages in Eastern Europe spoke similar languages, wore similar clothes. They shared customs and music and food. But their bonds went much deeper, child, because the people of those villages struggled together against poverty, disease and death."

"They broke bread together when there was none. They danced at weddings when lamentation was all around them. They worshipped in secret as entire villages were scattered. And slaughtered."

"I know many here suffered losses in Auschwitz and Dachau."

Though Mama never spoke of it, she and David knew about the women's camp at Birkenau. They would press their ears to the radiator pipes, listening to her pray at night. On most nights, her prayers were racked with sobs. Though she wanted to go to her mother, Magda always felt she was somehow to blame.

"It's normal for a child to feel guilty when a parent is upset. You should never blame yourself for your mother's tears, Maggie, she would not want it."

"Yes, Auntie."

"Now, let's see these letters."

Mrs. Hencz reached around on the chair to dig in her purse for her bifocals. She turned them out of their case into a soft palm, breathed on them lightly, and began cleaning them on the hem of her skirt.

"Let's put these in order by postmark."

Like a flurried game of Mah Jongg, the two women sorted letters out across the table. Mrs. Hencz reached for the oldest letter and began to read aloud.

Dear Eva,

My darling, I'm a dying man without you here to sustain me. I know there are no words that will right my wrong. There are also no words to describe the love I feel for you, my wife. I do not deserve you.

I beg you to forgive my transgressions as a husband. I never meant to hurt you, or our child. If I had known the pain this mistake would cause, I would never have been captivated by her.

All my love to you, my darling. Please forgive me.

Shimon

"Hmmm," murmured Mrs. Hencz. She opened the next letter.

Dear Eva,

My darling, I plead with you to reconsider the impact your decision will have on our son. I believe my namesake will become a leader for our community—with the love of a unified family.

Consider how your anger will ripple through time to our grown son. Who will raise him to manhood? Who will teach him? He will be set adrift by the hardness of your heart! I fear for him.

I am a man of God, Eva. In the time we've spent apart, I've become aware of evil forces at work. I believe that whore was placed in front of me to test my faith—a test I failed. I fear her wickedness will spread like an infection across future generations.

You are the shepherd. Have the faith to stamp out what has already begun. Do not let her destroy our family, Eva, I beg you.

Shimon

"You know, Magdalena, why don't I take these letters and try to make sense of them for you? I can call you tomorrow. I'm tired now."

"Yes, Auntie, I'll come back later."

Magda paused at the sight of the letters. She was afraid to let them out of her sight. Those letters held the answers to questions she'd long-feared. She didn't yearn for understanding. Just validation of what she already knew.

"Auntie, David and I believe Izabel was my mother. We aren't sure of my paternity, though these letters imply I was the illegitimate daughter of Izabel and Shimon. Why, then, was I raised by my father's wife?"

"Eva and Izabel lived in desperate times. I know Eva suffered great losses in Hungary. I also know when Izabel came to America; she was not embraced by our community. She was angry at her treatment by others who escaped here after the war. She was treated very badly. She had no family and no education. Only a misguided hope. I knew she felt betrayed. We all contributed to her condition.

Magda picked up on the slip.

"What condition?"

"Well, her mind slipped, child, she wasn't fit to raise children. Our community leaders took you away from her, but it was Eva who agreed to raise you as her own. I think Eva pitied her. She never could sit idly by and watch a woman be mistreated.

"I'm tired now, girl, let me get something to eat. Do you want to join me?"

"No, thank you, Auntie, I am meeting someone for dinner."

"Oh," with a twinkle, "does Maggie have a beau? Is he very nice?"

"Yes, Mrs. Hencz, he is nice."

She stopped at the door.

"A family is marked by love and devotion. Blood is strong. But a love between friends can be stronger. Many times it's our friends who lift us out of our despair. Nothing can sever such a bond between two women."

Magda returned across town to her home on Pigeon Hill. She kicked off her shoes and padded across the floor to the kitchen.

No calls. Where the hell is he?

She grabbed a glass of Merlot from a half-empty bottle in the fridge, scooped up her cat, and plopped down on the sofa to embrace another Saturday night solo-flight.

She wondered how a "community" could decide her fate; could decide her mother was unfit to raise her. Didn't Family

Services have to make such a decision? She felt anger at not having any choice in her own parentage.

I wonder if life would have been better with that crazy Gypsy. I doubt she'd have hated me any more than I was in my home.

Community. For some it was a great comfort, for others a terrible burden. Especially for a young, single mother from Eastern Europe. Why didn't they help her? What did she do that was so bad she would allow her daughter to be taken away from her? What could any human being do to deserve such a thing?

America is the New World; land of freedom and opportunity. It was supposed to be a safe-haven. Instead, her immigrant mother became the target of a whispering campaign, by others like herself, in her new land. Magda wished she could make amends for her mother's years of isolation—but Izabel was cold in the ground now for many years.

Magda had dabbled in different faiths over the years. The only place she felt right was at a tiny Baptist Church in the rural outskirts of her county. Magda had no roots, no family, and no children; she yearned to go wherever she felt new again.

The Pastor often quoted Hebrews 13:1-2, *"Continue to love each other with true brotherly love. Don't forget to be kind to strangers, for some who have done this have entertained angels without realizing it."*

How right he was.

Nine

Dumb-dumb stared out between the vertical blinds. Her mouth moved in a silent meow at the mourning doves roosting on the balcony. Sometimes she'd grow distracted by the snowflakes floating past her nose on the other side of the glass. David watched her from the kitchen table in between sorting through the stacks of paper. She meowed plaintively at him, begging him to open the sliding-glass door, just a little. Unhappy at being ignored, she whirled around to lick her tail angrily, flopping onto her back, daring anyone to come near.

David was amused by her tantrum. It was a welcome distraction from the paperwork staring up at him. He'd known private investigator Stillwell for years—trusted the man implicitly. They served together in the Marines from '60 to '68; David as a radar technician and Jack as a military policeman. It was Dave's good fortune to have Jack as his roommate, as he spent most of his eight-year stint either passed out on the stairwell of his barracks or in the back seat of his car at the E-club.

He had Jack to personally thank for never being disciplined beyond Level One Substance Abuse training.

He'd known a few jarheads taking prescription Anabuse under the watchful eye of the Department of the Navy, only to beeline back for a 12-pack puke-o-rama in their squad bay. Nasty stuff.

It was an ugly incident on Hollywood Boulevard with a 'he-she' that made David the joke of every Marine on El Toro, the Los Angeles Police Department and his sister in Chicago. In a drunken stupor, David decided to grab the thing's crotch, neglecting two very important facts. One, it was a man; with the strength and agility of a six-foot, 200-pound linebacker, and second, it carried a pink, ruffled parasol; a device that could be wielded as effectively as any standard martial-arts weapon. Which it was.

That little brain-fart cost him twelve stitches in the head, a weekend in lock-up, court costs, office hours and the dreaded Level One training. This was probably what first piqued his interest in the legal system—a pink parasol—though he doubted he'd include that in his résumé.

The investigative report was thorough. David wondered what juicy tidbits an investigator might dig up on him. His achievements were impressive enough to compile a fairly decent dossier: high school honor roll, student government, academic scholarship to Northwestern's School of Law. His pump overseas gave him credibility with veteran's groups and preferential hiring status at the state's attorney's office. David knew, however, that his dabblings into New York City's sexual underworld made him a non-contender for the bench or elected office. Even a mediocre journalist needn't dig too deep to uncover his after-hours recreational activities.

For a while he thought he may be bisexual. He loved to fuck and would do almost anyone. The nastier the scene, the more turned-on he became. He pursued carnal pleasure with reckless abandon. Early-on in the Marine Corps, he contracted a burning case of gonorrhea in the Philippines. A Navy doctor prescribed a regimen of penicillin without blinking an eye, sending him off to enjoy the remainder of his shore leave.

"Next ..."

David's aversion to condoms also resulted in his having to finance two abortions—one in the 2nd trimester. Then there was the genital herpes he picked up from the Latina at the titty bar near O'Hare. He even ventured into the world of internet pornography and chat-room hook-ups. He found the anonymity to be an ancillary perk.

He felt no remorse about his sexual escapades. The women were eager participants. He personally found the women of Thailand most intoxicating: so willing and limber. David continued to travel extensively, not in pursuit of cultural enrichment, but in search of the hottest poon he could find.

He later discovered that one of the negative side-effects of excessive stimulation was that he needed to up-the-ante in order to satisfy his lust. He couldn't get off on straight sex anymore. He found himself drawn deeper into a world of pornography, S&M and group-sex.

There was one thing David feared most about public exposure. His friend Emma. She was the most radiant woman David had ever known. He first met her at New York's Metropolitan Museum of Art. He was there to meet a woman he'd hooked up with on an internet chat room. He'd hoped for an afternoon fuck-fest; instead, he was mesmerized by a brunette studying a Degas. She was staring so hard at the painting she never heard his footfalls, and she gasped when he touched her to introduce himself. Later at dinner, she told David she had recently been "saved," and was saving herself for her bridal bed.

Nuts.

There was something intriguing about her. He never knew a woman that wouldn't screw him. And the quality of the screw usually correlated to his anticipated earning-potential. David didn't understand a man that lavished flowers and gifts on a female, only to go home at the end of the night with a raging hard-on and a handshake for his trouble. David's willingness to open his wallet increased with the coyness of the prey. An easy lay only rated a plate of spaghetti and a movie rental.

This simple fact of life seemed lost on his sister Maggie. David felt that Maggie was the only woman in the world he could be completely honest with. No matter how depraved his escapades, his sister never condemned him. She might call him a freak, or laugh at him, or scold him, but she never turned her back, or betrayed his trust.

A few times, David brought his whores home to meet Maggie. He'd watch their reaction to his sister with great interest. Sometimes they scoffed at Maggie in front of him. Sometimes they took special pains only to sling mud at her later. One former girlfriend even had the gall to call a friend on a pay phone in the hotel lobby to ridicule his sister. Long-distance, no less. David overheard her when he came down to pay the desk concierge. He banged her hard after they returned to New York and never called her again.

Emma was the only woman to meet Maggie on her last trip to New York. They laughed together like old friends, ganging up on David, teasing him mercilessly. The harder his sister laughed, the more despondent he became. Emma looked genuinely happy. The reality took his breath away.

He knew he was in love with Emma, but he also knew better than to infect her with his 'disease.' His sister's seal of approval made the disparity seem even more hopeless. So, he headed to the bathroom for a snort, polished off the bottle of Cabernet Sauvignon and floated far, far away.

David gathered up the papers and photographs and threw them inside his briefcase. He was meeting Emma for dinner and he didn't like to keep her waiting. Even when the date was arranged so she could share the gory details of her new lover. He always felt the urge to vomit whenever she blathered on about her bible-thumping boyfriends. He guessed they held hands, went on long, moonlit walks, close-mouthed kissed, and discussed the number of children they'd have. David doubted if this stroke knew that his girl's best friend was a Jewish man-whore. No matter, he would work stridently to make sure he soon found out.

David strode over to the sliding glass door and opened it wide for Dumb-dumb, who crashed into a chair beating a hasty retreat.

"Humph."

He locked up his apartment and headed down to the street to meet his cab.

David rapped on the bullet-proof glass for the driver to stop at the Wild Poppy on East 78th St. He ran inside for a mixed bouquet of tea roses, her favorite. He loved surprising her. She was so emotional, she cried spontaneously, and he felt very protective of her. David thought he'd experienced the complete spectrum of human nature until he met Emmy's heart. She was a miracle.

As his cab pulled up to the *trattoria*, David scanned the street for any sign of her. It was a crisp, fall night and Emmy loved the outdoors. Just as he suspected, she was perusing a newspaper stand on the corner. He paid the driver and stepped out of the cab. He watched her from the street. She was wearing a long red skirt and black wool pea coat. A 1928 locket swung seductively between her tiny breasts.

Last summer they saw a chick-flick at a cinema in Soho. As she was throwing popcorn at the screen, David impulsively reached over to snap open her locket. Inside was a tiny, black and white photograph of her parents on their wedding day. After a long, silent moment, David snapped it shut, and kissed her on the cheek. His love for her was overshadowed only by his fear of rejection.

He crept up behind her on the street and gently placed a hand on the small of her back. She smiled and kissed him before leading him back across the street to the restaurant.

"Emmy, try something different tonight," he told her.

Emma always ordered the chicken parmegiano. Though she wasn't a strict vegetarian, she rarely ate red meat.

"How about a nice bloody steak? It's great for your libido."

David was not in any mood to hear about her new boyfriend. He was feeling cranky and didn't mind letting her know it.

She changed the subject.

"How is Maggie?"

David had told her about his father's letters several weeks earlier.

"I think she's fine. Still dating that pud."

He stared at her hard.

"I'm still shook up at what you told me," she said. "How those two women must've loved each other—it's quite a remarkable story, really. It's unfortunate Magda never knew the woman who risked everything to save her. A shame it's too late."

"I've learned one important thing in my life, Emmy. It is *never* too late."

He snapped open his briefcase to remove the investigative report on the elusive Izabel Remény.

"I will see my sister happy again. Will you help me?"

Emma picked up a recent photograph of Magdalena's Rromani mother.

"Of course I'll help your sister. I would be honored."

Ten

Shimon pulled a strip of rolling paper out of his wallet and cupped it in the palm of one hand. He dug into a tiny leather pouch for a pinch of tobacco, carefully sprinkling it down the center of the paper. In a single, fluid motion, he rolled the cigarette, twisting up both ends tight, and struck a match to light it. He leaned against the sweet pine siding of his house, inhaling the burning smoke in one, long drag.

He was stalling. He knew it had to be done, but he was afraid. Afraid of being caught—exposed. His wife lay sleeping just beyond the outer wall. After thirty-six hours struggling as midwife for Izabel, she'd collapsed exhausted into her bed. Eva herself was many weeks into her own pregnancy. Her hands were beginning to swell and her feet ached painfully at night. He worried about her ability to carry the child to term.

Eva's sweet face kept a strangle-hold on Shimon's integrity. Though his shame ran deep, a confession would only ease his own guilt. He was a coward. Cursed. A man living a lie. He lived in fear each day that he awoke with a start. At the beginning, he was exhilarated by his fear.

He'd never felt more alive than when he was with Izabel. Her youthful beauty penetrated the numbness of his very existence, awakening desires in him he'd never felt before.

He confided all these things to his best friend Pieter, but Pieter didn't understand. He wept openly, begging Shimon to reconsider, fretting over the impact on everyone, except Shimon. Shimon wasn't upset by this; he didn't expect his friend to comprehend such desire for any woman. Pieter was an old man, married for more than fifteen years, with three grown children. His wife was happiest when he was leaving the house. Shimon doubted they'd been intimate in years.

Slowly, Shimon pinched off the end of the cigarette. He blew on it to check for live embers and placed it inside his shoe. Smoking was the least of what he would have to atone for. He pulled his wool overcoat up around his ears and shoved his hands deep inside his pockets before heading out of town.

A chill crept along his scalp towards his neck. The night was clear. He saw Orion in the north sky as he picked his way along the wheel ruts in the dirt road. The light of the moon lit his way. Still, he glanced nervously at the dark, hulking shapes of juniper and oak, casting their moonlit shadows onto the hard ground. He was glad to be outdoors where his head was clear. He felt himself suffocating in his own house. The air was heavy in the candlelit room where his wife breathed rhythmically in her sleep. When he leaned over her to kiss her goodbye, a tear slipped down the pillowcase beside her cheek. He blew out the candle, determined to see his daughter.

Shimon's guilt felt like a stone crushing down on him. He teetered between self-loathing and defiance. How could he hurt Eva—the one person with the power to stop him dead in his tracks or leave him speechless and ashamed—for his own sinful lust?

He saw the love she felt for him in even the most-menial household tasks. She stayed up late preparing his favorite dishes and desserts, and baked bread for him before the sun came up in the morning. He mentioned his liking for morning toast and tea early in their courtship; how this simple act of love by his own mother went unnoticed by her husband until ill-health no longer permitted it. Eva picked up the torch, tirelessly baking for her husband, as generations of wives before her. He knew her profound grief at leaving home at such an early age. The loaves of bread were often seasoned with her salty tears, but Shimon thought those especially sweet.

Eva kept a tiny herb garden outside the kitchen. One evening at dusk, they stood inside the doorway, laughing, while an entire family of rabbits tucked in for supper. When Shimon rolled chicken wire over wooden stakes the next morning, Eva seemed sad to steal the tasty greens from the furry interlopers. He didn't know whether to laugh or scold her. Instead, he held her for a long moment, stroking her hair, before returning to his work.

Simple touches of elegance graced his home wherever she lingered. Roses cultivated from her mother's garden, antique lilacs grown from grandmother's cuttings; everything had some special meaning. Nothing was set down by accident. Even the simple iron cookware hanging in her kitchen held stories of afternoon visits with a Gypsy fortuneteller near her home in Villány.

Even though she surrounded herself with her cherished treasures, Eva often left to visit her mother. Although Shimon disapproved, he wasn't fool enough to forbid it. He almost wished her gone now, in order to ease his own mind, but their family physician advised against extended travel. Perhaps if Eva hadn't been at her mother's so many months before, he wouldn't have strayed from her bed. It was something to consider.

He turned off the main road to follow a path that wound along the river. He was glad for the frost in the air as it eased the biting flies that swarmed in the river bottoms. He felt a sudden urge to bolt when he sensed the overhanging tree limbs reaching out to strangle him. He blindly thrashed his arms about to free himself, ducking low to avoid the spiny branches that licked at his face and neck.

The path isn't so menacing by day, he thought to himself. It seemed like the earth itself knew him—the liar and thief—and it mocked him on his way to his lover.

He did love her. Just the sight of her thrilled him in ways he never expected. He felt drunk in her presence. Even now, at full-term, he felt an overpowering desire to be with her, though for months it seemed that Izabel struggled against him. She spent more and more time with Eva, hurrying away before he came within sight of the yard. Shimon knew her love for Eva had grown. They acted more like sisters than friends. He watched them chase each other around the vegetable garden with caterpillars, squealing like little girls. They tended each other's hair in the mornings and giggled over scandalous English novels in the afternoons. Shimon didn't care for such books, but the girls were a united front, and his protests fell on deaf ears. Lately, he almost felt unwelcome when he came through the door at the end of the day.

Shimon only tolerated this injustice because he was thrilled to see Izabel. He wished it were Izabel running to greet him, to embrace him and kiss him on his lips. But she always waited patiently for him to take her tiny hands in his and kiss her gently on the cheek. For the past few months, she refused him, choosing to offer her hand instead. Her defiant refusal to be touched, her indifference, only inflamed his passion even more.

She was the forbidden fruit, although the fruit should be offered willingly, and Izabel was becoming more distant every day. An overwhelming sadness now crept over her when he lay with her in one of their secret places. Sometimes she cried, sometimes she sat in stony silence, sometimes she rejected him altogether. No matter, he loved her more with each passing minute, and she whispered the same when they parted.

He wondered if her growing love for Eva would temper her desire to be with him. The possibility almost excited him. It was exciting to love someone when any careless thing could turn you on your ear. Shimon relished the edge they teetered over, but Iza did not. He didn't care. He'd long-since passed the point of no return. Nothing— not his wife, his parents, his community, his God—could convince him that his very breath didn't depend on her.

Her pregnancy did little to temper his lust. It was not an ideal situation, but Shimon felt confident he could care for them both. He convinced Izabel to go to her parents and throw herself on their mercy, concocting a story of a rape by an unseemly village boy. He knew enough of her culture to know that he'd spoiled her for marriage. He secretly reveled at the thought of having her all to himself for as long as he cared to. No man would accept her and her parents would be grateful for Shimon's support of the fatherless child. Eva would have her 'little sister,' the children would grow up under his watchful eye, and he would appear the benevolent caretaker of poor, downtrodden women. It was seamless. No one would be hurt. He would seek absolution from God with his care of the child.

In the back of his mind, he recognized his twisted logic. He knew he would destroy Eva, shame his family and be cast out of his community. Whatever remorse his libido didn't suffer, a snifter of wine handled nicely. Eva remarked on his moodiness, and excessive drinking, but she trusted him implicitly. Never would she consider his awful secret. Her mind was not able to grasp such treachery. On this he counted...and prayed.

Around a bend in the river, he came to a clearing where a solitary wooden shack had been hastily built for the birth. As a pregnant Rromni, she was considered *marime*—defiled and impure—by her community and ordered into strict isolation. The allegation of rape would be considered later by a *kris*. This group of men would determine whether she should be cast out entirely from Rromani society.

Her quarantine only allowed her limited contact with her mother and a designated midwife. She could only touch essential household objects, which were collected by the women throughout her confinement to be destroyed. This included cooking and eating utensils, sheets, and clothing soiled by the touch of her hands. Shimon found the practice senseless and barbaric, so he gave no resistance to Eva's pleas to remain by her side.

Shimon came within a few yards of the primitive shanty and listened. It was deathly quiet. He became fearful and drew closer, whispering.

"Izabel, it's Shimon, may I visit for awhile?"

Many minutes passed without a sound. Fear enveloped him as he started for the door, when it opened a crack, and she said, "Come and see your daughter, Shimon."

He entered the tiny shack and waited while his eyes adjusted to the gloom. She swept past him to a tiny bundle of rags lying in a nesting box on the floor. She plucked up the newborn child and deposited it unceremoniously in his arms. The baby was red and wrinkled, with a head so pointy he laughed aloud. Angrily, Izabel moved to snatch the child away, but Shimon said, "No. Not yet."

He gently pulled away the swaddling cloth and touched her soft, bare skin. She was perfect. The baby was long and thin, not yet fat from her mother's milk. Her hair was a shining mass of black curls atop her head and her eyes were open wide, staring up at Shimon's face. Her lips sucked the air and her fingers curled into tight little fists. He gently pushed his thumb inside a tiny palm. She grasped it tightly and moved her lips as if to cry.

Shimon began to shake uncontrollably. In heaving sobs he prayed to God, begging his forgiveness, and for the protection of his daughter. He could never deny her. Her eyes and lips were his own. His mother would need only a glance to recognize this as her grandchild. For the first time in his life, Shimon felt fear and dread. What had he done? He glanced over at Izabel, patiently waiting for him to finish before speaking.

"Shimon, you are her father. I will never deny you to her. But I will never lay down with you again, for you've made me an outcast of my own people—the only ones that may have loved her as their own. Her name will be told you at her baptism in two-week's time."

"She will never know you. She will grow up to be strong and wise and she will lay waste to the shameful curse you've put upon my family.

I love you. But I know I can never have you, so I don't want you anymore."

Izabel wrapped the infant in clean rags. She removed a long, straight pin from her skirt, took his hand, and pricked the inside of his wrist. He stood silent as she squeezed droplets of blood onto the child's bunting—formally recognizing Shimon as the father in the Rromani way.

"You will not visit us again after sunset, Shimon, for your coming draws evil spirits, the *tsinivari,* which could attack us during the night. Only Eva and my mother will be allowed to protect and care for us while I am *marime*.

"You are no longer welcome here."

Izabel sat down on the soft dirt to prepare the child to nurse. She hummed softly to her as she wiped the dried blood out from the creases in her ears.

"She will be baptized in two-week's time. You will not take your anger out on me by forbidding your wife to come to me.

I am not afraid of you. Do not take away the only person that loves me. I warn you, Shimon."

Shocked, Shimon backed towards the door. He held out a tiny gold amulet. "A gift," he stammered. He placed it on the floor, turned, and fled. Once she could no longer hear his heavy footfalls pounding down the dirt path, Izabel leaned over to retrieve the amulet off the floor.

Nested inside was a tiny, handwritten scroll with the verse, *"the sun shall not smite thee by day, neither the moon by night."* Izabel took the pin she had used to prick the hand of her lover to fasten the amulet to her daughter's swaddling. She bared a swollen breast so her daughter might take nourishment.

"You will live, Magdalena. You will live and you will have the strength of my spirit to help you live," she said. Then, she closed her eyes to rest.

Eleven

"What is this woman doing here?" Eva was shocked to silence when Izabel's mother burst into the tiny room. Her nostrils flared open wide as she glared at Eva with absolute derision. *She looks as though she's caught wind of some foul odor hanging in the air,* thought Eva.

Eva glanced over at Izabel lying on the straw mattress, clutching at her stomach, for a cramp was growing again deep inside her. Eva had assisted many of the *hameyaldot ha'ivriyot,* or Jewish mid-wives, near her home in Villány. She knew there was only mild abdominal pressure early-on, not unlike what she would expect during her monthly menstruation. Soon, though, a squeezing and tightening in the small of the back would follow. If the mother were lucky enough, there would be several hours of labor, but if she were unlucky, it could stretch on for days. After that, came the period called "transition," a sickening shifting of bone and joints, when the child's head rotated down through the birth canal.

Eva watched as Izabel explored the taut skin on her ripe belly. "Eva is family, mama. She is here to help."

"Your family is asleep in your father's house. I do not know this woman."

"Yes you do, mama. This is Eva Szótemel. She is the wife of the scholar at the Jewish Temple in Mártély. She is teaching me to know English. She is very well-educated." Izabel's face beamed with pride.

"Well-educated?" Eva detected a slight sneer on the woman's lips.

"Please don't embarrass me, mama!"

"Tell me what this educated woman knows about treating a skin rash with weeds along the roadside? Can she prepare a tonic to cure a stomachache? Does she know how to cool a burn, or disinfect a sore, or close a wound?"

"You're just jealous, mama. You can't stand that I have a friend."

The old woman's lips drew a thin, hard line on her deeply etched face. "Could she scratch a living with her own hands and feed a family on it? Will she sew your child's clothes, prepare her milk, keep her clean, and fed, and dry?"

"You're acting like an ignorant Gypsy. You need no help from me; you're doing a fine job yourself." Izabel groaned aloud as a fresh wave of pain swept over her. Eva gazed over at her friend—uncertain whether to stay or go.

"Do not insult me, daughter."

The old woman's gaze did not waver. Izabel's eyes fell to the floor.

"You waste your time, Izabel. Will reading books help you to raise this bastard of yours? Or will we ignorant Gypsies be left to clean up your mess?"

Eva interrupted the old woman. "Grandmother, I *am* educated enough to know that I am not welcome here."

Eva turned to her friend on the floor beside her. "I don't want to interfere, Iza. You are in good hands with your mother." In a pleading voice, she whispered, "Please don't fight with your mother, Izabel, it's not right."

Izabel rose up on her elbows, barely able to speak, for another contraction had seized her. "She's not leaving...*you* are."

The old woman's eyes grew wide with surprise, then narrowed again. "I see you've learned no manners from your teacher. What wisdom have you gleaned, then? How to disrespect your mother? Or break your father's heart? Or dishonor your people by lying with strangers?"

Izabel's eyes began to fill with tears. "I told you I was raped!"

Eva raised both hands in the air, palms outward, in the global gesture of reconciliation. Her tongue felt as dry as spun cotton. "Grandmother, I don't think it is good for Izabel to get upset in her condition."

Izabel's mother turned her full attention to Eva, speaking to her with resolute authority. "I am truly sorry if I've offended you, Madam. But you should not be around my daughter while she is *marimé*. She requires special care, as does her child, if they ever mean to return home.

If they are found unclean by a *kris*, Izabel and her child will be cast out of our community. They would not survive for long."

Eva noticed the woods outside had grown strangely quiet, as though the birds in the trees were listening to the rise and fall of the voices inside. All that was left to fill the palpable silence inside the room was the crying of the wind against the shutters.

"Go home, mama. I no longer care about your community. I just want my friend here with me now. Why can't you understand that?"

"What a fine daughter I've turned out. And what about your father?"

What Eva saw next made her blood freeze like ice in her veins. Izabel stared vacantly at her mother; inky black orbs glittering across the room. The flickering candlelight danced on hollow cheekbones and sunken eye sockets. She looked demonic and grotesque—a gargoyle—and for an instant Eva did not recognize her. She dropped her gaze and looked again, only to find the same unrecognizable face. Her eyes looked empty to Eva; devoid of light, and hope.

Eva's heart pounded in her chest. She fought the urge to flee. She knew something was terribly wrong, but she was frozen in place.

. "Would you feel the same about me if papa was the father?"

A death pall came over the old woman. She stood on broken eggshells, staring across the room at her daughter, shell-shocked and silent.

"Don't look at me like you didn't know, mama. Really! Like you haven't known for years." Izabel seemed to smile at the ridiculousness of it.

"You've always hated that papa loves me more than he loves you. You are old and afraid. Go home, mama. You had your chance to protect me. There's nothing you can do for me now. Go home."

Eva gulped in shallow breaths of air and her legs twitched convulsively as she waited for Izabel's mother to come unglued.

The old woman shut her eyes. She crossed her arms around herself in a giant hug and rocked back and forth.

"You are a whore. I knew what you were even as a child, Izabel. Your father's never harmed you, daughter, except to indulge your every whim. How he spoiled you— the daddy's girl! I watched it for years. And now you try to manipulate us by shifting your blame back onto me? Own your shame, girl! You've earned it."

Izabel screamed incoherent Rromani curses at her mother as her tiny fists pounded on the worn mattress. Her neck turned a dangerous shade of purple. "Get out, get out, get out! You bitch, get out! Get home to papa!"

Izabel's mother snatched her shawl off a nail on the far wall and threw it around her shoulders. She was furious. Her hands trembled violently and her lips stretched white across her face. Eva expected the old woman to strike Izabel, and so was prepared to throw herself upon the girl.

The old woman paused just outside the door to look back at her daughter lying on the floor in a crumpled heap. "I am your mother. That is a bond that can never be broken. I think I will leave her here."

She placed a wooden statue of the Blessed Mother gently on the dirt floor.

"Perhaps she will help you to reflect on what suffering it is to be called 'Mother'."

Izabel sobbed uncontrollably. She pressed down on her stomach with both hands, seeming almost to be straining against the coming child.

"And think hard before you make another accusation against us. You are still a Rrom, with all the ugliness that implies, and you will forever be despised by all who look upon you. You and your child will return to us. We will be waiting for you to bring her home."

Eva stared in disbelief at the slammed door. The primitive walls reverberated once and then fell silent. Eva crawled across the floor to her friend. Izabel's face was turned from her. Eva could only see the back of her shoulders, rigid and motionless; except for an occasional shiver.

"Are you cold?"

She shook her head no.

Eva moved closer to sweep aside her hair. Compassion washed over her like the rain through a sun-scorched desert.

"I didn't know, Izabel. I'm so sorry."

Suddenly, Izabel spun around to face her. Her tiny mouth trembled as she spoke.

"There is much you don't know about me, sister. I'm afraid if you knew everything, you may never speak to me again."

"This is not your fault. And *that* was not your fault. And there's nothing in the world you could do or say to me that would make me love you less. Don't be a goose! Now lie down and rest while I read aloud."

Izabel curled up on the floor beside her while Eva read to her about Antigone - the Greek woman who murdered her beloved children to spite the man she loved. She thought to herself, *how could Izabel fear the loss of my friendship? I wonder what other secrets she is hiding.*

Twelve

Izabel's sobbing permeated the room as she unfastened the bobby pins holding together her daughter's soiled diaper. She used one corner to wipe away the solid waste while reaching for a pail of water on the floor beside her. She wrung out a cleaning rag and gently dabbed at Magdalena's inflamed bottom. The infant screamed in pain as Izabel tried vainly to remove the mess from her skin, finally using a jagged fingernail to scrape away the remnants.

"I'm sorry, child," she cried, reaching to steady the tiny legs flailing about in agony.

Magdalena was several months old now. Her cries had increased in their intensity and pitch; her tears flowed out like the waters of the river Duna. Her tender skin was streaked with blood from a staph infection that had turned the flesh white, then gray, then scarlet red. Izabel's mother had left her a lard-rendered salve, but nothing helped.

In desperation, Izabel folded up the child's legs and dipped her genitals into the pail of cold water. Little Magdalena paused for a moment, gazing up at her mother with a look of surprise, then inhaled one long breath to protest her indignation. "Damn him," Izabel swore. She deposited her daughter roughly back onto a wool blanket amid a chorus of fresh screams.

Izabel bawled as she smeared greasy ointment on her daughter's sore skin, bitterly cursing all who had abandoned her. For many weeks she'd not seen Eva. She knew her friend had given birth to a son. Her mother told her the child's arrival had been heralded throughout the countryside, even meriting mention in a newspaper in Pest. She tossed the clipping onto Izabel's lap several days earlier.

Halachist Shimon Szótemel of the Temple Harzion and his wife Eva are proud to announce the birth of their son, David Joshua Szótemel, born April 28 at home in Mártély. Grandparents are Ben and Rose Remény of Siklós and Joseph and Sarai Indulat from Villány.

"You would have thought this child of royal blood; a direct descendant of Prince Árpád himself," Mama said. "How jealous you must be at her son's reception. It is an interesting turn of events, for certain. You must be curious to see the little prince. I guess she is still exhausted from her labor."

Every day her mother brought her the latest gossip, serving it up like a tender blossom with the afternoon tea. She seemed to relish rubbing her daughter's nose in her humiliation. Izabel suffered the daily onslaught with enough indifference to negotiate the news while discouraging further ridicule. She gobbled it down like sweet kernels of corn, hungry for the agonizing updates, while inevitably being sickened as they took root in her heart.

Her persistence led Izabel to wonder if she suspected her granddaughter's paternity. She knew her mother's eyes missed little; it wouldn't surprise Izabel if her cruelty ran so deep. Her life had indeed become hopeless; she need not be reminded.

Izabel endured lonely days in the shanty with her child. Her only visits were from her mother on the afternoons when she finished her washing. Although Izabel still awaited her judgment by the *kris*, her mother seemed in no hurry for their return home.

"There is scant room in your father's house. I don't know how we'll find an inch for my little Magdalena."

Mama straightened the baby's nightdress and brushed loose strands of silky black hair behind her tiny ears. She fussed over the child in a way that Izabel had never seen before.

Izabel wondered if this was some misguided attempt to seek forgiveness for not protecting her from the sexual advances of her lecherous father. After Magdalena's birth, his depravity was never brought up again. But the old woman's actions spoke louder than words—she would never allow harm to come to Magda—Izabel was certain of it. Iza was not even sure if she was still *marimé*. It seemed their isolation might be a deliberate attempt by her mother to keep them isolated from her father. She asked her mother, point-blank, that afternoon.

Her mother sighed deeply as she prepared Magdalena for her nightly bath. She carefully slipped the child's bedclothes up over her head, nuzzling her soft hair against a wrinkled cheek. She clicked her tongue in disapproval of the horrible infection on Magda's privates. The baby screwed up her tiny face as she was laid in the warm washbasin.

"We will let her skin soak awhile in the warm water," said her mother. Grinning up at the old woman, Magdalena kicked a fat foot to splash water onto her grandmother's worn apron, then giggled with delight at her grandmother's open-mouthed expression of surprise. Even Izabel smiled, despite herself.

"Mama?"

"Truth be told, daughter, I am afraid for your return home, but not for the reasons I'm sure you're thinking."

She glanced at Izabel for a moment, saying, "You never believe anything I say. You think I don't love you. It's always been this way between us. I only hope you'll someday realize my love for you. A mother's love. You should understand this now."

Izabel stared at her in disbelief. Though her shoulders were still rigid, tears began filling her eyes. Izabel was touched by the sincerity in her voice. Her heart wept.

"Times are terrible for our people in Romania, Iza. Rroma registered by the government are being rounded up and taken to labor camps. Many men have left for work, never to return home; many have been dragged out of their beds in the middle of the night. We do not know where they are taken. We think them all dead. It is a travesty.

She paused as if wondering where to continue.

"There have been witnesses that the women and children in the camp in Varsand were thrown into a shallow grave and shot. They were covered over with dirt. Some of the people buried under the bodies were still alive. Their muffled cries were heard by a passing farmer who dug them out. Women and children!

She clapped her hands over her face.

"I am afraid for our people. It is rumored that the Jews watch us, feeding information to the Romanian Iron Guard Legionnaires to save their own families from the death squads. Policemen? They are butchers!"

Izabel stared at her mother in disbelief. She'd left many friends behind in Varsand. She never dreamed of not seeing them again.

"Why were they murdered, mama?"

"I don't know." She abruptly shifted her focus. "Her water is getting cold. Time to dry off my little *chírilo*."

She lifted the soaking child out of the washbasin onto a clean towel. She rubbed the baby briskly while her little chin trembled in the cold air.

"Add more wood to the stove, Iza, your daughter is cold." Her mother pulled a light in close to inspect the girl's behind. "Hmm."

The old woman removed a square of waxed paper from a hidden fold in her skirt. On it laid a glob of gelatinous liniment which she slathered onto the exposed skin.

"This is a poultice of flax seed and elm bark. You must apply it every few hours. It will heal her sores."

The old woman then rubbed a finger, dipped in brandy, over the infant's gums to calm her. "You must have such pain, Magdalena. This will ease your suffering."

And it did. Her fiery red skin turned dark pink. She cooed up at her Nana, enraptured, much to Izabel's chagrin.

Why does she do everything better than I? She even takes better care of my child than I do. She glowered jealously at the sentimental scene before her.

She stood up to fetch the books borrowed from Eva, and flipped through the pages, distractedly looking for her place. The books left a bitter taste these days; the words rang hollow and meaningless. She was lonely. She longed for the companionship of her tutor. She missed her friend.

"Perhaps I will visit Eva this afternoon," she murmured.

"Haven't you heard a word I said?" Her mother's angry outburst prompted Magdalena to burst into tears. "It isn't safe, you stupid girl! We are being hunted. Thousands have died or gone missing."

Then, she tried a gentler approach. "You are safe here. Stay out of town and away from camp if you want to live."

"Watch my daughter." Izabel pulled a sweater up over her head and straightened the braids under her *diklo*.

Her mother darted across the room to lunge for her arm.

"No, Mama. I want to see her."

"She doesn't want you around. She doesn't want you around her husband. I think we both know why. Don't play stupid with me. I knew the moment I laid eyes on him he had designs on you. The Jewish bastard! I don't think Eva is so stupid not to know of the affair."

"Shut up!"

"Has she once visited you, or your daughter, since last December?"

"Shut up!"

"She knows!" Then, more quietly, "She knows. And since she knows, what would stop her from reporting you to the authorities?"

Izabel tried vainly to pinch some color into her pale cheeks.

"I'm begging you not to go. I can protect you here. Your secret is safe with me, daughter. I am afraid you will leave your child an orphan."

Izabel brushed her lips against her daughter's crying face and walked out the door.

"Izabel!"

The air felt good on her face. It had been weeks since she'd last ventured outside the vicinity of the shack. The anticipation of seeing her dear friend hastened her steps along the footpath.

Trees swayed gently in warm spring breezes and clouds rose fluffy and white against blue skies. Butterflies performed an erratic dance among the wildflowers swimming in high grasses along the edge of the tree line. Water fowl cried overhead, searching for a place to rest for the night. Izabel breathed in deep breaths of the delicately scented air.

It was good to be away. She loved her daughter, but the incessant crying infuriated Izabel. In her darkest moments, Izabel considered flinging the screaming infant out into the fast-moving river current. If she wrapped the blanket with heavy stones, no one would ever know her awful secret. These murderous impulses were compounded by a residual sadness that never left her heart after her daughter's birth.

No matter how desperate, Izabel always laid the baby down to race towards the river, alone, breathless with the desire to silence her daughter forever. How many times had she wanted to smash her tiny body against the walls of the shanty? Izabel's fury and isolation held her in constant shame. She thought these things as she picked her way along the riverbank towards the town. She was eager to share her feelings with Eva; she knew her friend would somehow understand.

Izabel heard men's voices upstream. Her eyes narrowed and, crouching low, she slunk into the tree line to scout their location. She'd learned the art of concealment—how to silhouette herself against a tree or disappear into a field—at an early age. She never thought it strange; it seemed natural, like a game. The adults taught the older children to scatter whenever strangers drove up on a campsite; the women disappeared inside with babies still suckling at breasts.

Slowly she crept forward. She spied a small group of *gajikane* squatting down along the river, talking together in loud voices. They were strangers to her, although she knew them to be Magyar from their dialect. They were dirty—their faces mean.

Like a shadow, she quickly moved for the cover of the dark woods. She wondered if the men were the police her mother had spoken of at the shanty. She knew such men were paid puppets of the Nazis. They were scum to Rroma because they were traitors to their own people. Open treachery and disloyalty would never be tolerated by the Rromani people from one of their own. Such men would certainly be found face-down in the waters of the Duna in time. With never a witness to be found among them. She did not understand why the Magyar people tolerated abuse by traitors.

She moved through a strand of birches, turning north to mirror the curve of the river. Her pace quickened in her excitement to see Eva. It took less than twenty minutes for her to come within sight of town. Eva lived north of Mártély, in the Jewish sector, in a tiny blue cottage surrounded by plantings. Roses, lilacs, home-grown vegetables and herbs—her garden hummed with life. Izabel thought it heaven on earth.

Izabel nearly ran through the south yard when she noticed a celebration underway inside her friend's house. People milled about the kitchen against a candlelight backdrop. She stood outside the window in the fading light and saw Eva and Shimon's extended family, as well as the temple elders from Harzion. Several prominent businessmen from neighboring Hódmezö-Vársárhely sipped cordials, smiling at the young girls serving food to guests.

Feeling shy and self-conscious, Iza felt an urge to turn back home, but she screwed up her courage, and stepped up to the kitchen window. As she was about to knock on the door, Mrs. Sarai Indulat's face rose up like a catfish in the paned glass. Her eyes narrowed in recognition of the Rromani girl. She covertly shook her head at Izabel while laughing at some unintelligible joke. Her eyes never broke their icy stare. Iza's face burned white-hot as she stepped forward to rap briskly on the outside door. The catfish looked around to see if anyone heard her knock, then rushed forward with a look of angry determination.

"What do you want?"

"Could I please talk to Eva, Madam?"

"She is busy right now, Izabel. Can't you see Eva is entertaining guests?"

"May I please see her?"

"No, Iza. Where is your child?"

"She is at home with my mother." Izabel flushed with the pride of new motherhood while Mrs. Indulat glanced around with unfeigned disinterest. "Yes. That's very nice. Shouldn't you be getting back home to your child, Izabel?"

"I want to see Eva. Now!" She stomped her feet impatiently on the ground. Mrs. Indulat gently shut the door on her face.

Izabel peered inside. A group of men stared at her through the window and whispered among themselves. Izabel turned on her heels and blasted towards the main entrance. She wrenched open the front door and stormed past the invited guests to the living room, where Eva sat with her newborn son.

"Eva?"

Eva's head shot up, eyes open wide.

"Oh, hello, Iza."

Iza's smile faded as she waited for her friend to jump up in her customary greeting. They stared at each other without speaking. The silence was deafening. Shimon bellowed at her from across the room.

"How the hell did she get in here?" He glared at his mother, who shrugged her shoulders at her son.

He aimed his sharp eyes at Izabel. "This is a private celebration, Izabel, a religious celebration, you are not welcome here."

"I'm here to see your wife." Her eyes remained locked on Eva while the infant in her lap began to squirm.

"My wife is caring for our son. This is more than I can say for you."

Izabel turned to face Shimon, who shrank beneath her gaze.

"Don't you mean to ask who's caring for *our* child, Shimon?"

The men in the kitchen snickered at the allegation. The women's hands flew to their mouths, gasping in horror, secretly watching for Eva's reaction.

"*Get out of my house!*" Amid the terrible din sat Eva, silently observing her husband. She laid her son into the arms of another and rose to head off his enraged charge.

She stood in front of Izabel, holding up her hand against Shimon.

"Stay away from her. If anyone should leave this house, it should be you, Shimon."

Then she turned to Izabel.

"Please leave, Iza. I will come to see you in a few days. We will talk about this at that time."

Izabel whipped around her to snatch the infant out of the arms of the distracted guest. Audible gasps filled the house as she held the child high in the air.

"You are not alone, little one. There is another. She will never be acknowledged by anyone here, but she is of your flesh and blood, and I will teach her to love her little brother. And despite the struggles of those here, you will rise up out of the sin and deception of your father and you will recognize and love your sister ten-fold. Your happiness will depend on her happiness. This is how it shall be between you in the time to come."

She nuzzled the child against her cheek and returned him to his mother.

To Shimon she said, "Your sins shall not fall on your son, for the spirits of the earth will protect him now. They will fall on your head like a great tidal wave."

And to Eva, "Your absolution remains in removing yourself from this man, for he will bring great suffering on those around him for the remainder of his days."

Shimon grabbed her by an elbow and threw her out into the darkness. He slammed the door behind him and hissed at her.

"You're dead to us. Touch my son once more and I will bury you. Don't ever come here again."

Thirteen

Sarai knew with a certain sense of irony that, as in Jerusalem more than a thousand years before, the birth of her grandson in 1941 coincided with a national census in Hungary. At that moment in time, Hungarian Jews numbered 725,000. *725,000.* The birth of David filled her heart with anguish.

Shimon told her that all around them in neighboring Ukraine, Czechoslovakia, Romania and Yugoslavia, the Germans had already decimated millions of European Jews. No one was safe. Neighbors turned against neighbors. The flames of bigotry and hatred exploded into a fiery inferno and her people were being roasted alive. Her spirit trembled with the knowledge that David would not likely live to see his fifth year.

Shimon's words were tinged with dread as he patiently explained to Sarai that the "Third Jewish Law" that defined the term "Jew" on more radical racial principles added 58,320 persons not belonging to the Jewish faith. The numbers of Christians of Jewish origins far-exceeded this estimate. Now, 850,000 persons were officially registered as Jews by mid-1941. They were now marked for disposal. It was only a matter of time before the devil came to collect his due.

Word trickled down to their village about the sadistic methods used by the Nazis to exterminate Jews. Sarai's husband, Joseph, often sat on the front porch in the early evenings after supper, taking watch as the earth prepared to slumber. As a student of history, Joseph was well-versed in human atrocity, but his studies could not numb the pain of knowing each day brought evil closer to home. Joseph stared out at the creeping darkness, wondering what might happen upon his doorstep in the night.

Joseph never shared with her any of the news whispered in meetings with other community leaders. She was sure he hoped to spare her an agonizing wait. But Sarai also had a tight-knit network of spies. Wives, lovers, and confidantes—all with insight into the lives of the men whose beds they shared. The information she managed to gather was quite disturbing.

The Nazis had begun their smear-campaign years earlier. Jews were deemed "Christ-killers," in league with the devil, accused of desecrating the Host. Blood libels perpetuated the widely-held belief that the drinking of Christian blood was practiced in Jewish religious rituals.

Sarai was horrified to learn that the Nazis also promulgated the "science" of Eugenics, which theorized the positive modification of "Social Darwinism," or natural selection through selective breeding of human beings. So was born the ideology of "racial hygiene" by Hitler. *How could one human being be born so evil?*

The practice of Eugenics meant little to those of Aryan ancestry, but any person of undesirable genetic makeup required cleansing. Those considered genetically "unfit," "defective," "useless eaters," or "life unworthy of life," must be eliminated.

The shitting out of the world's "asocials" wasn't enough, thought Sarai. *We are as rabbits to a pack of wolves. They tear at our flesh and devour us alive as we scream silently...praying for death to overcome us.*

Shimon once studied the ideologies of Martin Luther, who wrote of the impending destruction of the Jews in his *On the Jews and Their Lies*. In his book, Luther advocated a program to arrest Jews, expropriate them, force them into government labor and, finally, exile and murder them. Almost 400 years later, the Nazis implemented Luther's blueprint. The cleansing had begun.

~ * ~

The methodology used in implementing Luther's blueprint was measured and systematic. In 1932, the Nazi party publicly refuted forward-thinking art and aesthetics. Then in 1933, political demonstrations were banned in Germany. This was followed by a presidential decree that gave Chancellor Hitler emerging powers. Dachau, the first concentration camp in Germany, was soon established, the first of more than 1,000 by 1945.

The stranglehold tightened as German Jews were choked off from the outside world with boycotts, unemployment and economic sanctions. A law restricting enrollment of Jews in schools was passed in 1933. Less than two weeks later, books deemed of "un-German spirit," mostly Jewish, were burned opposite the University of Berlin. Works by Mann, Marx, Hemingway,

Sinclair, Wells, Freud, Proust, London and Remarque—20,000 in all—were burned to ashes.

Then the government began to regulate newspaper publishers. Political opposition to the Nazi Party became punishable by law. A codicil that stripped newspaper editors of power over content soon followed. First, clamp down on the ability to freely communicate. Then, ban freedom of personal expression. Next, impose economic hardship and dependence on the state. Instill fear and doubt. Intimidate the leaders. Enact laws to weaken defenses. Soon they are numb to the horrors that await them.

The Germans secretly enacted laws that provided for the sterilization of "unfit" parents and potential parents, compulsory castration of "hereditary" criminals and the euthanasia of the "defective. Little was known about these secret programs as the German News Bureau was established to feed propagandist news to Germany's newspapers. The killing of innocents seemed contrary to the declaration by Reich Chancellor Hitler that he, himself, was a member of the Catholic Church, particularly with the later amendment providing for compulsory abortion of "unfit" fetuses up to six months in utero.

From 1933 to 1939, more than 1,400 anti-Jewish laws were passed, and special Nazi courts were established to deal with political dissidents. Homosexuals, Catholics and Freemasons were all persecuted in earnest by Nazi thugs. Worst of all, German churches collaborated with the Nazis by supplying records to the government, indicating who was, and was not, a Christian.

In defiance of the Versailles Treaty, the Rhineland was the first to fall to German occupation.

At a political rally in 1937, Hitler announced the Third Reich would last a thousand years. At the same time, Hungary's own Ferenc Szálasi established the Arrow-Cross Movement dedicated to anti-Semitism.

On May 29, 1938, Hungary tried to appease the Nazis by restricting the proportion of Jews holding jobs in commerce, industry, the liberal professions and the government. As a reward for Hungary's declared alliance with Germany, sections of Slovakia and the Tran Carpathian Ukraine were annexed by Hungary.

Back in Germany, any Jew "previously convicted" of a crime, even a traffic offense, was arrested. Germany cancelled the licenses of Jewish doctors and barred lawyers from practicing in Germany.

On March 11, 1939, Hungary enacted a law permitting the establishment of the Hungarian Labor Service System. Jews of military age would be employed in construction, mining and fortification work for the military.

Falling to Nazi Germany in 1939 were Austria, Sudetenland, Czechoslovakia, Lithuania and Poland. In May 1939, Jewish participation in the Hungarian economy was restricted to 6%, and restrictive laws were passed against Jews engaged in law and medicine.

Forced labor, coerced shaving of beards, destruction of property, beatings and forced dancing all served to publicly humiliate Jews throughout Europe. They were forced to clean latrines with their bare hands. Mass killings in the forests of Poland had begun in earnest.

The mistreatment of Poland's Jews accelerated as Germans seized businesses, homes, furniture, currency, bank accounts, art, and jewelry. Now economically helpless, Poland's Jews had nothing to sustain themselves. Mass murders of Jews, the mentally ill, the elderly, the physically ill and handicapped in Poland were rampant. Next to fall were Denmark, Norway, Holland, Belgium and France in 1940. Dictator Ion Antonescu assumed power in Romania in September of 1940. Eastern European Rroma fell victim to sweeping relocation and extermination policies as the German Air Force began to attack British targets.

On January 21-24, 1941, Romanian Iron Guard Legionnaires launched a coup d' etat, during which anti-Jewish violence boiled over. On April 2nd, Hungarian Premier Count Pal Telecki committed suicide rather than collaborate with Germany after accepting the largely Romanian region of Transylvania in the summer of 1940. The Germans invaded Greece and Yugoslavia soon after.

Though Hungary never embraced its alliance with Nazi Germany, the association brought significant new territory, and the comfort that Hungary wouldn't suffer a German invasion. Sympathies toward the Nazis increased following Soviet bombing attacks on Hungarian targets, prompting Hungary to enter the war, joining the Axis powers, in 1941.

Immediately the government rounded up 18,000 Jewish refugees and deported them to the Ukraine. All throughout the Western Soviet Union, Lithuania, Romania and Latvia, mobile killing units murdered men, women and children in retribution for unknown offenses. Beatings, random shootings, fatigue, hunger, thirst, exposure and disease were rampant on the marches to the internment camps.

On August 27-29, 1941, nearly 25,000 Hungarian Jewish forced laborers were shot to death in bomb craters near Kamenets-Podolski, Ukraine.

German infanticide was rampant. This was no mere attempt to break their spirit—these child killings were much more sinister. The Germans drowned thirty Jewish children in clay pits in the Warsaw Ghetto. Jewish boys were cornered on the streets by soldiers, who forced them to expose their genitals to check for circumcision if they looked Aryan.

Word arrived from a Rabbi in a neighboring Soviet village that a killing squad had machine-gunned all adult Jews and covered them over with lime. Not wishing to waste bullets, the soldiers seized the children by the ankles, smashing their heads against walls and roads. Many others, too young to walk, were buried alive with their parents in the lime pits.

Allied victories in every hamlet prompted the Nazis to hasten deportations. Hitler publicly declared the war would mean the destruction of European Jewry.

The tide turned for good when an encircled German 6th army surrendered to the Soviets at Stalingrad, Russia on February 2, 1943. From this point on, most of Europe believed the Germans would not win the war.

"The only way to help the Jews," the Allies maintained, "is by an Allied victory." However, Allied victories only seemed to torment the beast. It gorged on the feast, sensing its impending doom.

Not all European nations buckled beneath pressure by the Nazis to deport their Jews. Bolstered by Allied war efforts, Bulgaria defied German demands for Jewish blood. The Bulgarian government resisted, thanks to the ambivalence of the nation's king, as well as protests by clergy, farmers and intellectuals.

No matter. By the spring of 1943, two million Jews had already been murdered by Nazi killing squads throughout Eastern Europe. In true form, Hungarian regent Admiral Miklos Horthy met Hitler in Austria in April of 1943. Hitler encouraged the deportation of Hungarian Jews. Horthy refused to acquiesce.

Degrees. Infinite, imperceptible, degrees. Acceptance occurs in degrees. After months of refusing to turn over its Jews to work as slaves in Yugoslavian copper mines, the Hungarian government finally acceded to German demands.

On October 20, 1943, the United Nation War Crimes Commission was established. Bolstered by Allied victories in Italy, Romanian dictator Ion Antonescu ordered his cabinet to resist German efforts to exterminate Jews in the Transnistria region. This was no coincidence. Antonescu was a coward, though self-preservation did little to help him in the end.

In March 1944, German forces invaded and occupied Hungary. German control placed 725,000 more Jews directly into German hands. In May 1944, deportations of Hungarian Jews to the Auschwitz death camps begin in earnest.

~ * ~

Death. So much death. Sarai envied the dead that they were put out of their misery. Death was coming for them all, and sooner than they knew. She sensed it.

Like a rabid wolf, its mind wracked with fever, Sarai felt death approaching in her dreams. She heard the low rumble of its growls. She saw it lurching as it entered the yard, its diseased eyes trained on her grandson lying helpless on the grass. The wolf rushes in, snarling and insane, tearing at his tender, white belly.

I am old. Joseph is old. I pray to God to save David from what is soon to come.

Fourteen

One never gets used to it...being alone. There must be some evolutionary reason human beings aren't adapted to a life of solitude.

Humans are amazing creatures. They can adapt to the most difficult life situations. Convicts learn to appreciate the creature comforts available in prison. The aged find solace in the rhythms and structure of a nursing home. Children who've been abused resist attempts to place them in foster care.

They adapt. They survive. Such is the reason the species has managed to thrive in a hostile world. The hallmark of human civilization is marked by a dependence on others. People yearn to make connections. They ache to be known and loved, unconditionally, by other human beings. Such is the basis of marriage itself, to be united in flesh and in spirit, connected and unbroken, working together to defend hearth and home.

What happens to the Canadian goose that does not have a mate come winter? She is hard-pressed to find food, shelter, to defend herself against predators. All take a heavy toll on her resources. She is vulnerable. Her flank is exposed. She may even welcome death. Her struggle over, she finds peace.

There is great wisdom in a herd mentality.

Magdalena reflected on these morbid thoughts as she sipped her Chai tea and watched the birds fluff themselves over the feeder in her forsythia bushes. They made such a racket it was hard to think. She smiled at a fat mourning dove gorging itself on the tasty morsels showering down on the snow.

There's the smart one.

It was hard to snap out of the black once it enveloped her. Christmas was just a few weeks away. Her brother hadn't been home in months; busy on some new project, a blonde bimbo, she supposed. Whatever occupied his time these days seemed to fill him with renewed vigor.

She was disappointed. She hoped a spark would fly between Emma and her brother. Emma was the only woman her brother had introduced her to with a modicum of class and more than two brain cells to rub together. With Magda's luck, he'd end up marrying some skank from Brooklyn. She could spend the holidays listening to them cursing over the jellied cranberries. Or maybe she could prepare a sumptuous Sunday meal while her brother's evil offspring set fire to her cat. She shuddered at the thought.

No family. Few friends. She needed to get a life. Depression does that. It isolates you, chokes you off, like a cancer restricting blood to the heart, leaving you utterly alone. Depressions, illness, anger, fear…all block out the light. All are relationship killers.

When Magda first cut loose from her obsessive relationship with Paul, she felt giddy and dizzy, elated and exalted, convicted and powerful.

Yes! I finally scraped the shit off my shoes. Good for me. I am strong. Powerful. Fear me, dastardly men.

Her conversations with casual friends helped boost her confidence, pump her self-esteem, until finally she'd gathered enough courage to...

Change her phone number. *Hiiiya!* Oh, yeah, and make it unlisted, too. *Eat that!*

Her swagger soon faded much as her friends did, for they were no longer cheerleaders, they were now life support.

Clear!

She required heart massage and electro-shock therapy daily. She was a walking nightmare. The whole lot of them lost Magda's number in a hurry when she dared try and impose on their plans with significant others. Like a puff of smoke, they were gone.

She didn't blame them. She was a coward and she knew it. She didn't even have the courage to tell Paul why she deserted him. He'd made an anemic attempt to contact her at work, then quickly lost interest. Easier conquests to be had elsewhere, for sure. His light-speed journey back to the dating scene, casually mentioned by coworkers over lunch, sent her self-esteem crashing back down.

"I guess he really didn't love me," she sniveled.

I guess the brick he threw in your face, the one with the note on it that said, "I don't love you, Magda. I only have room for one person in my life. Me. You were simply a distraction while I waited for someone better to come

along," didn't quite sink in. Guess you never got that memo, girlfriend.
Someone prettier. Thinner. Smarter. More elegant. More successful. *Just more, stupid! I bet a guy like Paul would've lost his mind over someone like Mama. No. She was too refined for that dirt-bag. He only pursued grateful women.*
Never mind. Magda could now focus all her attention on the mystery that surrounded Izabel. Mrs. Hencz had been translating the letters for her for months, but there was no new insight into her mother's choices. She did learn that Eva had become pregnant again before she forced Shimon out of the house, but there were no clues as to the whereabouts of the child.

Madga wanted to visit Eva's gravesite to determine if there were any children buried near her mother. A tiny infant could easily be buried over another family member in an unmarked grave—a practice common in those days. Many children died of disease and malnutrition during the war.

She would pay another visit to Mrs. Hencz. There were questions she still needed answered that could not be explained away by a stack of faded letters. The old woman was hiding behind them, evading poignant questions about what happened after Izzy came to America. Madga refused to be assuaged or distracted. She would get her answers. If only the old woman wouldn't cry; how she hated that!

She wished David were there to help. But, it was *her* mother, why would he care? David had the perfect mother, but he could also be ruthless, especially with anyone from the 'old neighborhood,' and she doubted a few tears would deter him.

Magda didn't understand all the secrecy. What was Mrs. Hencz hiding? Did she play some part in Magda's fate? She wondered. Who was she protecting? Magda? Herself? Or others?

Madga finished her tea and rinsed out the cup in the sink. She slid on her yellow boots and tramped through the snowdrifts to refill the birdfeeder. Birds quarreled on the overhead telephone lines: sparrows, blue jays and a ruby-red cardinal. The fat mourning dove waddled under the peony bush. He peered out at her from beneath a snow-covered branch, believing if he kept perfectly still, Magda would never notice him.

Madga headed back to the house, stretching to follow her tracks through the snow. She came to the back door and stomped the snow off her boots. Her teeth chattered as her frozen jeans began to melt against her skin.

She ran upstairs to pull a hairbrush through her black mane. She pulled the loose strands out of the brush, rolling them into a ball, and then added it to a growing mass in her top dresser drawer. She once heard that if you released your spent hair outdoors in the spring, the birds would use it as nesting material. Madga liked the idea of baby birds lying helpless in a cocoon of her black hair. Warm and comfortable. It would probably be the closest thing to motherhood she'd ever experience.

She waded through a pile of clean laundry on her closet floor for an outfit. *I'll be lucky if I can squeeze my can into this.* She pulled out a conservative, purple dress with long sleeves, and black leather pumps. She would take her mother's old friend to lunch today. Neutral ground.

God help me to know the truth.

She pulled open the ironing board, filled up the iron's water reservoir and waited for the steam. Max wound himself around her legs and meowed plaintively for a treat. She tried to shoo him away with one foot, but he was a male with attitude.

"If you eat anymore, I'll have to send for a zoologist, because I'll have created a new species. *Gigantis Felinus.* Shoo, Max."

Madga pulled the dress down over her head and, kicking aside the black leather pumps, pulled on more-comfortable boots.

I can only stand so much pain today.

She grabbed her purse, threw on her coat, and slammed out the front door.

She raced across town, not from the desire to see Mrs. Hencz, but with resolve to get the answers she needed about the two mothers in her life. The one who had her but didn't want her and the other one that had her but..."

I'll have six of one; half dozen of the other.

She crossed the Fox at Indian Trail, glancing downstream at the homeless people lying along the riverbank beneath a strand of trees. Had Aurora always been so ugly? Garbage was strewn along the shallows beneath the viaduct. A policeman slammed his car door, hiking up his belt, and moved in the direction of the vagrants.

Let them sleep, she thought.

Get drunk and sleep. Sounded like heaven to her.

She arrived at Mrs. Hencz's house and immediately noticed the shades drawn tight.

Had she gone out?

She parked her vehicle and crunched through the snow to the front door. She rang the bell. A fat, orange tabby perched in her bay window meowed plaintively at Magda through the glass. She rang the bell a second time and watched kitty twist himself like a pretzel to get a better look. She was just opening the storm door to knock when a head popped out of the house next door.

"She's not there."

"Oh."

Magda paused. "Do you have any idea when she'll return?"

"Can I help you with something, young lady?"

"No, ma'am. I was just supposed to pick up Mrs. Hencz for lunch."

"Are you her family?"

"Yes," she lied. The old woman softened.

"I see. Well, I don't know what time she'll be back, but I do know where she went off to."

Silence.

Magda was growing impatient.

"And where would that be?"

"She's having lunch at the Rheinlander Club. Maybe she wouldn't mind an unexpected visit. I know I wouldn't."

Was that a glint of meanness in her eye, Magda thought. She shrugged it off and, thanking the old woman, moved off in the direction of her car.

The Rheinlander Club was founded by the first German immigrants that followed 'Industry' to Aurora around the turn of the century. It wasn't far, only a few blocks due east. She arrived at the club in ten minutes despite the snow and the rush of last-minute shoppers, and parked adjacent to Mrs. Hencz's car.

When she first walked into the club, her eyes took several minutes to adjust to the dim lighting. A jukebox polka rang out over the noisy lunch crowd. Old men sat at the counter drinking tall glasses of beer while reading the newspaper. Waitresses bustled around the counter with plates of warm sandwiches. The smell of sausages, sauerkraut and dumplings filled the room. Madga's mouth watered. A memory, laced with sadness, struck her as she pictured Eva preparing similar dishes in their kitchen long ago.

She stood for a moment, dazed, and then noticed a table of white hair waving at her. Was that a look of dread on Mrs. Hencz's face? Or was it annoyance? Perhaps she was mistaken.

Maggie watched Mrs. Hencz turn to the man next to her and whisper something in his ear.

"Did you forget our lunch?"

"Oh. Ya, ya, ya. Sit down, Magdalena. Join us."

"I thought you were avoiding me," she joked. No one cracked a smile. They all studied the soggy pickles and limp lettuce cups left over from lunch.

"Sit, girl," ordered Mr. Loucks, "We hear you've been asking Alice here a lot of questions about Izabel."

Mrs. Hencz smiled wearily. The old man put his arm around her protectively.

"What is it you want to know?"

The hair went up on the back of Magda's neck as she smiled and said hello to Mr. Loucks. She was determined not to engage the entire neighborhood in her personal business.

Pieter Loucks was the man who monitored all the neighborhood kids from his front window; a self-appointed neighborhood watch, long before any such thing even existed. Her brother had spent hours riding his noisy big-wheeled tricycle up and down the sidewalk in front of Mr. Loucks' house.

"You, there. Boy! Get off of the street. Where is your Mama?"

"I'm not on the street," David shouted back.

"Don't smart off at me, young man. I've known you since you were knee-high to a grasshopper."

"Yah, yah!"

"Don't smart off at me, boy. Where's your Mama?"

"In your butt. Ya, ya!" David jeered at the old man.

Mr. Loucks started out across his yard for David.

"Leave him alone!" Magdalena shouted at him from her perch in the great ash overhanging the sidewalk.

"Quiet, girl! If you were a better sister you'd not let your little brother ride his tricycle in the street. Why, if a car didn't see him, he'd be road-kill, and it would be *your fault*," he said.

"Worthless girl. Back in the old country, if an older sister was caught not paying mind to her younger siblings, she would get a thrashing!"

"Shut up, old man. Go back inside your house and leave us be."

Inevitably, Mama heard the ruckus and came outside to investigate.

"Hello, Pieter, how are you this morning?"

The old man seemed to deflate two sizes when Eva addressed him. Most men did when mama's eyes fell on them. They were enchanted.

"Good morning, Eva," he stammered.

"And a beautiful morning this is, indeed. Have you ever seen the sun shine so brightly?"

She shielded her eyes with her tiny hands and gazed off at the cloudless horizon. Mr. Loucks followed suit and, nodding enthusiastically, admired the brilliant blue sky.

As he gazed up at a midday star, Eva turned to call them.

"David. Magdalena. Come in for supper!"

Mr. Loucks pushed his hands deep in his pockets, scowling at them as they passed.

"That girl of yours needs to learn to respect her elders, Eva. These children should be taught our ways. They are becoming lost and confused in this land without culture. That one, especially, needs to be reminded how to behave as a proper Jewish girl."

"Heathen," he muttered under his breath. David stuck out his tongue at the old man from behind his mother's back.

When mama stepped into the kitchen, she paused to look at both of her children seated at the table, her eyes flashing with anger.

"Don't listen to him, Magdalena. You *are* special. More than you even know. You will one day rise out of this town to fulfill your destiny. I sense greatness in you."

"David is my heart, but you are my soul. Don't you ever forget that."

She never did.

Mr. Loucks still had the hardness about his face. He was a very old man now, his face lined and gaunt. But his eyes were unchanged.

Like a rooster in a henhouse, he was surrounded by the town matriarchs. Ruth had long, white hair and brilliant blue eyes. She had lost part of her right foot to diabetes, but her cooking could still bring tears to a grown man's eyes.

Ruth's apron pockets were perpetually filled with candy. She had a gaggle of kids forever hanging around her yard or bumping on the porch swing. Ruth was foster grandmother to all of Aurora's street urchins. It seemed to Magda that she was Mother Goose, Mother Hubbard and Mother Teresa—all wrapped up in one—to the dirty, unfed and uneducated of Pigeon Hill.

Sarah sat beside Ruth at the table. Sarah was the neighborhood tart. She looked fifteen years younger than her actual age. She had strawberry blond hair, unusual for a Jewish lady, and sultry green eyes. She was petite with a large bosom.

Sarah liked to sunbathe in a bikini in her front yard, although her husband built a beautiful deck with an enclosed fence, and planted privy hedges along the side of the house, in a vain attempt to relocate her away from the street. Teenaged boys flocked to her door, whether or not her own son was home. The visits continued long after her Frank left to attend university.

Like nectar to a bee, men adored Sarah. She needed to be the center of attention. She often struck up animated conversations with busboys and doormen when her cup was feeling a little empty.

Next to Sarah at the table sat Josef, known as "the bachelor," who lived a few doors down from her. Josef was missing most of his right arm. Fascinated by the dexterity of his stump, Magda ogled at him from behind her window curtains as he trimmed his shrubs or mowed his lawn.

Josef had a collection of pornography in his garage. He'd even been so kind as to let her look at the graphic pictures, once while he watched her from a shadowy corner of the garage. Mrs. Hencz came storming in a few minutes later, yanking her outside by her collar, ordering her to stay off of his property.

Magdalena was fascinated by this dark and mysterious Hungarian. He'd once married a girl, much younger than himself, but the woman disappeared after less than a year, and he soon became the neighborhood recluse.

Magda well-recalled the many others who'd long-since passed. Gene Meszaros lived in the house that backed up to Madga's back yard. A few feet from the alley he'd planted a tremendous vegetable garden with lettuce, onions, corn, beans, cucumbers and decorative cabbages. He even planted a few pumpkin vines for her and David each Halloween.

Gene could grow tomatoes the size of a man's fist. David and she used to find the biggest, most-grotesque tomato caterpillars crawling along the cedar shingles on the garage. Grotesquely thick, green, with soft black hair and protruding red stalks, they looked like some weird alien life form.

Also vivid in Magda's memories was Mrs. Yeager, the wife of the town drunk, who lived a few doors down with her gaggle of dusty children. Her husband got work at Thor Power Tool on Claim Street and had moved his family up from Kentucky. Magdalena became fast friends with the oldest daughter, Bibi, with whom she'd long since lost touch.

She would never forget Bibi. Bibi was an American beauty, with flaxen-blonde hair, light blue eyes and pale skin. Her brilliant smile could light up a room. She later heard that Bibi's older brother Bobby was serving a stint at Joliet Correctional, but she never learned what became of her friend. Pressure from the Aurora police forced them to move after only a few years.

David claimed to have seen Mrs. Yeager raking leaves with a much-younger boyfriend in front of the homeless shelter on River Street a few years ago, but there had been no sightings of her since. She apparently had no teeth and looked 'rode hard and put up wet' as David would say.

Madga pitied her and the thousands of other women like her. She was only one or two bad choices away from it herself.

"Poverty is not a crime," she chastised her brother. But if Bibi's misfortune had led her down the same path as her mother, if that wasn't a crime, then what the hell was?

The five sitting at that table were all who remained from her old neighborhood up on Pigeon Hill.

"I do have something to ask you. Actually, I'm glad everyone's here, because I suspect that this pertains to everyone here. I want to know how I came to live with Eva. Why didn't I grow up with Izabel?"

"Only for the grace of God." Pieter let out a malevolent snort.

They all laughed nervously.

"Dear, we all think you had a lovely mother. You've grown into such a beautiful young woman," said Ruth.

"Yeah, I'm confused, Magda. I fail to see your problem," said Pieter.

Sarah lifted a finger to her lips. "Shush."

"My problem is you," said Magda. A hush fell over the table.

My problem is that I cannot squeeze an ounce of truth from your tired old asses.

"Please help me to understand. I have no living relatives except David. The truth lies in the graveyard along with my mother. I implore you to search your hearts and tell me what happened."

Mr. Loucks' face quaked with anger.

"You speak to us about *your* loss? We don't know what it is to feel pain? Every person who sits before you lost loved ones in the war. Some were taken from us before our very eyes. You forget yourself!"

"Quiet," said Sarah. "Magdalena, forgive him. Pieter lost his family over in Hungary during the war."

Ruth attempted to explain, "We came here to America. We only had each other. We came as strangers to this new land and found families in our neighborhoods. We eked out an existence and helped each other survive."

Mrs. Hertz chimed in, "We helped Izabel survive also. She came here with nothing but the clothes on her back and you two children. We gave her food, clothes. We helped her with you children. Pieter got her a job in his bakery. You were all starving. We did not know how she came to us, only that she was on the brink."

Pieter, his face an angry mask, barked, "How dare you accuse us! You insolent girl."

"I'm sorry," she mumbled, "I wasn't accusing anyone."

"That's right, you should be sorry."

Ruth hissed, "Shut up, Pieter. She has a right to know. We have no right to keep secrets from Magda. She is Eva's girl. Eva would have wanted her to know."

"Piss on Izabel. I spit on her grave. I hated her then and I hate her now. She was evil. Wicked. But let this girl know. I'm sure it will do her good to know her mother was a murdering whore. Yes, I'm sure it will heal her broken heart to know these things."

Ruth cried, "Shut up, you old goat."

Pieter grabbed his overcoat with shaking hands. He stormed towards the door, but not before shaking his fist at the table. "We all agreed twenty-five years ago we would not speak of Izabel again. We would let the horrible secret between Eva and Izabel die along with them. Let what is dead stay dead. This will not help the living." To Magdalena he said, "You want the truth? Bah! I have seen 'the truth' destroy marriages, families, communities and churches. Hope is what you will extinguish with your precious truth."

Pieter pointed a gnarled finger at the old women. "The truth will cut this girl down. She will writhe on the ground with you old bitches wailing and wringing your hands over her limp body. How many generations must suffer for the sins of one? Let it go, for pity's sake! Righteous miscreants like you need something to justify the disease that lies dormant in your own hearts," he hissed at them. "Bah!" He growled, his rheumy eyes popping out of his skull, and he shook his fist one last time before storming out the door.

Magda sat down in the old man's place and faced her unwitting adversaries. "I will not leave this place until I know the truth. Tell me what my heart yearns to know, Aunties. I beg you."

Mrs. Hencz gazed down at her wrinkled hands before she spoke. "Yes, Magdalena, we will tell you everything. The sun will not set on one more day without the truth told to our daughter. We are old. The time has come." The others nodded in agreement.

Maggie began to weep. Mrs. Hencz took her hand and began to speak.

Fifteen

Near the ancient seaport of Varna, along the shores of the Black Sea, an early-morning dew clung deep inside the shivering husks that withered, papery and prostrate, in the baking summer heat. As the shadows grew long, a storm gathered on the horizon and thunder rumbled low in the sky. The fiery dragon moved fast across the prairie flats, breathing out its scorching breath, a hint of rain in the taste of it.

A farmer looked up from the harvest to study the thunderheads gathering in the southwest. Spinning cloud formations dissolved into larger ones and the sky glared down at the earth, which sighed and whispered beneath it. The farmer tipped back his straw hat, scratching at the grit in his hair. The corn danced in the shimmering heat, seeming to call in the rain.

The farmer stood at the edge of the field. He felt a cool blast on his face and heard the rustling of the cottonwood near the water well. His wife called to the green-eyed girl still playing with her dog along the creek bed. The woman yelled at her husband to help her as she slammed out the screen door to gather in the wash. He ignored her, watching the great sheets of rain, several miles across, sweep over the dry earth, lightning flashing sideways across the greenish-black.

"Nikolai," she hollered.

"*Az Isten Szerelmére!* Are you coming in?"

"Go on ahead. I'll be there in a minute."

Come on, you bitch. Bring us rain.

He felt excitement building in his chest. Another cool breeze licked the skin of his face and he pulled off his hat to catch the chill. A wild gust marked the sudden arrival of the storm, sweeping his hair up, evaporating his sweat instantly. He stood alone, feeling strangely alive. His nostrils flared as he breathed in the raw smell of ozone and felt the hair on his arms tingle with the charge coming up from the ground. He opened his mouth to catch the first drops, savoring them as they slid down his throat.

Sixteen

David snapped on his headlamps and accelerated the Porsche to eighty miles an hour. He was late. He was always late. The meeting with his latest client ran long. He hated divorces…they were so ugly. He'd never heard of a divorce that didn't involve a third-party. Lucky for him he hadn't been tangled up in one himself. Yet.

He had a special place in his heart for married sluts. They were so damned grateful. Like throwing a bone at a starving dog, then watching him choke on it.

Though he didn't exactly specialize in divorce law, he'd occasionally get a call from some poor schmuck whose wife was boffing a coworker. It was all so cliché. He was astonished at how much two-timing was actually going on. Even the most fresh-faced, clean-living couple had skeletons in the closet.

David was beginning to think that sex was America's national pastime. If you weren't getting it, you were plotting on how to get it, or despairing over not having gotten it. When did these people find time to work? Take care of the kids? Mow the lawn? Walk the dog?

All excellent ways to sniff out sexual partners.

Maybe my perceptions have become jaded. Maybe I only see what is evil in this world. The spirits of the dead can only see the dead.

Loose living had taken a heavy toll on David's heart. He felt it, hard and brittle, in his chest. He wasn't happy—he was cynical. Self-indulgence, pornography, indiscriminate sex, alcohol and drugs, seasoned with a complete absence of conscience, were not happiness. They were hedonism.

Maggie said that we lived in a fallen world. Hell if that wasn't true. She'd tried to get David to come with her to church a year ago. He was shocked; they had been raised Jewish. When had she gone to the other side? He was a Jew, he was proud of his Jewish ancestry. It was his heritage.

He figured Magda probably didn't share his attitude about their childhood. She was a square peg trying to fit a round hole. Always was. She never felt the love and nurturing he enjoyed at home. Though he had abandoned the traditions of his parents, he knew he could break the glass in case of emergency. Judaism was his safety net.

He never doubted his faith. He never doubted God's love for him. She could have her Sunday church services. He understood what it was she was seeking. He knew her. He understood her pain and heartache. She was searching for that which David already had: unconditional love, acceptance, and hope for the future. Each was mired in his own stinking shit. Each absorbed in his own struggle with the demons that chased them all the way from Pigeon Hill.

He was only now beginning to see his salvation would begin with his sister. He now had a function; a purpose to his life. He'd never thanked her for being second. Her acceptance of this role assured him the cream of life; she consumed what was left with no complaint. He loved her more than life itself. More than himself. She was his best hope - he sensed it. She could turn to Christ if she wanted, but he had other plans for himself.

He'd thought he had time: time to find the right woman, time to return to temple, time to clean up his life. Then, in the blink of an eye, he found himself rounding middle age. He was driven, focused, and tenacious in his search for truth. He was almost there now.

He could barely contain his excitement, but all the loose strings had to be tied before he would share the news with Maggie. He wouldn't disappoint her. She deserved a history. A lineage. She deserved the truth.

David rounded 113th and slowed to a respectable crawl. He didn't want to draw attention to the speeding black Porsche, having no desire for an early Chanukah gift, compliments of the New York Police Department. David was supposed to have been at the apartment an hour ago. He was afraid to call Emma for fear she'd already left.

They'd planned to go to a midnight screening of *Casablanca*. *Gag*. He couldn't believe he'd actually agreed to this. He didn't even have the excuse he was pussy-whipped—he'd never been there, or done that, with Emmy. He guessed it was true guys would do nearly anything just to be in the vicinity of good poon. You never knew when you might catch a whiff of it on the air. The fragrance made him salivate.

David's love life was dry as a California desert. His mind was occupied with Izabel's investigation. Detective

Stillwell had pulled a few strings at the State Department and produced a complete background check on Izabel. Magdalena often welcomed Brett into their home on lonely holidays when they were still in the Corps and Brett never forgot a kindness.

Seemed the U.S. government was also keeping tabs on the movement of the elusive Gypsy. Izabel wasn't dead. Just missing in action. The amazing thing about Rroma was their ability to disappear altogether. Over the course of a history marked by persecution, they had mastered the art of blending into the background.

Stillwell called late one night with news of Magdalena's mother. "Hey, shitbird."

"Hey yourself, butt-ugly. Did you find anything yet?"

"Finding Izabel alive was the easy part, my friend. Finding her is another ball of wax altogether."

"I don't follow."

Stillwell snorted over the phone. "Now, why doesn't that surprise me? Show me a state-school graduate with a law degree and I'll show you someone who wasted six years of college."

"Fuck off, man."

"You'd like that, wouldn't you, pervert? Well, it seems Izabel left Aurora in a hurry."

"Why's that?"

"Can't say. But here's the best part, Szótemel. After a short stay at Mercy Hospital for a "nervous breakdown," Izabel was released to the care of none other than…well…you take a guess."

"My mother?"

"That's right! How did you know?"

"Must have been the six years I wasted in college."

My mother and Izabel. What was the story with those two women? David scratched his chin stubble thoughtfully.

"And that's not even the best part, shitbird. Izabel checked *herself* into the hospital. Though her inpatient records were sealed, I don't think she was too disturbed, she was only prescribed an antidepressant.

David quipped, "Won't Magpie be pleased to discover her mother wasn't a noodle short of a casserole."

Stillwell paused for a moment. "Brother, I interviewed one of the nurses at the hospital who remembered Izabel. When I asked if she knew what became of Iza's two children, the nurse thought they were placed in nearby foster homes."

Funny, neither Magda nor I have any memory of this.

David knew his father's friend Pieter, who first arrived in Aurora in 1945, played some part in Izzy's swift departure. Pieter's home had become a halfway house for others who chose to travel to the Midwest for a fresh start. Pieter Loucks was a pain in the nuts to the neighborhood kids. But the old man was caretaker and father to nearly every Hungarian Jewish family that settled there after the war.

So, why not help a single mother with two small children?

David turned his attention to parallel parking his baby a few feet from Emmy's building.

Like butter.

He jerked on the hand brake and leaped out; admiring the sleek line of his vehicle. David ran his fingers through his hair and checked his breath in his hand before ringing the apartment buzzer. Nothing more was required. He knew he looked good.

Emma never even bothered to speak over the intercom before buzzing him inside. She was far too trusting. Like most New York attorneys, David had the pleasure of working with many of that fair city's scumbags. Hell, he was one of them!

She was like a child in that she had to be constantly reminded how to keep safe. "Emmy, you shouldn't buzz me in without first making sure I'm not some random weirdo."

Her smile was already weakening his resolve. "And how do you know all the men I buzz in are random weirdoes? Maybe I was expecting them."

He sighed, "I know you don't check before you open the door for me."

Her Irish eyes sparkled. "Well, that's because you're the only friend I have left, David. You've already slept with most of my girlfriends, and the rest you've managed to scare away with your ubiquitous charm. Thanks for that, by the way."

David rolled his eyeballs at her, "You're welcome. Now, as long as we're discussing your utter lack of self-preservation, why is it you insist on identifying yourself to callers?"

Her smile widened, "I didn't know we were discussing this. I thought *you* were discussing it. I'm just sitting here listening to your rant."

David rapped on his leather briefcase for emphasis. "Stay off the street at night, Emma. And while you're at it, park your car closer to the storefronts."

Why do I worry about her so?

He stepped into the elevator. By the time he reached the seventh floor, he'd hatched a plan to teach her a lesson. He tiptoed to her door and, instead of knocking, pressed his body against the outer wall, being careful not to make a sound.

He waited for several minutes, then, just as he was about to give up, he heard the sound of lightly tapping heels on linoleum flooring. Like a badger, he flattened against the wall. The hall was quiet and empty. He knew she was peering through the peephole.

As she jiggled the deadbolt and scraped the chains, David pressed his entire weight against her door. As soon as the locks sprang loose, the door flew open against his 200 pounds, throwing Emma backward onto her entry floor. She yelped when he covered her head with the hood of her sweatshirt and pressed a hand against her mouth.

Her chocolate lab, Lady, barked excitedly as David playfully dragged her toward the living room by a long, slender foot.

"Goddamnit, David, you scared the Bejeesus out of me!"

She kicked at him with her one remaining foot as he laughed uproariously at her on the floor. "You (kick) scared (kick) the shit out of me (kick, kick, kick)!"

He rolled on the floor in convulsions—until he saw her standing over him in tears.

"Emmy, I'm sorry! I just wanted to teach you not to let strangers into your building. What if this happened to your neighbor with the two small kids?"

"You're such an asshole," she cried.

She stormed to the sofa. Feeling slightly ashamed of himself, he went over to join her, but she continued pouting, arms crossed in front of her.

Jesus, I really scared her. It was freaking hysterical, though! I am an asshole, Emmy. I'm glad you noticed. Except that it makes this so much harder for me.

He gently tried to lift her, but she jerked her arm away from him. "Don't play that gung-ho, Jarhead shit with me, David. I'm not one of your dumb Marine buddies. I am a grown woman. Treat me with some goddamn respect or don't come around at all."

He smiled at her, ignoring her harsh words; he'd never seen such anger in her before. He persisted tugging at her, ever so gently, and finally she rose to meet his embrace, bawling like a wounded calf. "You scared me. That was not funny. It was a mean thing to do. I don't know what's wrong with you sometimes, David."

He pulled her tiny body against him, feeling her heartbeat against his ribcage. He softly kissed her hair. "I'm sorry. I'm sorry. I'm sorry. It was cruel. I know I play too much sometimes. Forgive me, Emmy. You know I love you like a sister."

He swallowed hard. "I love you, Emmy."

She jerked away, wiping her eyes, then turned to fetch her handbag.

"I know. I know. And I love you like a brother. Now let's get out of here before I change my mind. Chinese or Italian?"

He was shaken by her nonchalance, though he'd heard it before. As soon as they got caught in an intimate moment, one would shove the other away. He was resolved not to back down. Not tonight.

He'd had enough of being her buddy. He was ready to declare his intentions. Best he do it here. If she rejected him outright, he could forgo dinner for drinks at the corner juke-joint. Why risk public humiliation if he could stake his claim in privacy?

She rummaged through the fridge. She came up for air with a tinfoil-covered can of dog food to distract Lady while they snuck out. He swore that dog was like a kid. Its feelings actually seemed to get hurt when they left her home alone. Not like his cat, who cycled between catatonic and psychotic. He stood next to Lady while Emma scooped.

"Emmy?"

No response.

"Emmy?"

"Please don't."

"Don't what?"

"Don't say it, David. I like where we are. I like my life. I am comfortable. Happy. Doesn't that matter to you?"

"Of course it does."

"Then don't."

He reached out to touch her. She didn't stop him and she didn't move away. He gently lifted one hand, then reached for the other.

"Please, David, no. I love you. You are a great friend. But you'd be a shitty boyfriend."

He smiled down at her and pulled her towards him.

"Don't you think I know about the women, David? I know all about your lovers. You are a cad. I can't be with a cad."

He stopped dead in his tracks, hands frozen in mid-air. He didn't move a muscle. She stood toe to toe, her shoulders back, defiantly throwing the gauntlet at his feet.

He saw a tear trickle along the fine hairs of her skin. His hand swept down to catch it as it pooled on the edge of her chin.

"Say what you want about me, Emmy, nothing is going to scare me away. I'm not going anywhere. Try all you might, I'm here to stay.

Gazing at her, he ran his hand through her hair. "I love you Emmy. I've loved you from the first moment I laid eyes on you. You are perfection to me. You are the only thing in my life that makes breathing worthwhile.

She looked at him in amazement.

"My world is gray without you, Emmy. Please don't take that from me. I couldn't stand it."

He held her tiny hands against his chest. "I love you, Emmy. I want you at my side. Marry me. I swear I'll be a loyal husband to you."

He cupped her chin in one hand and kissed her tenderly on the lips. She sobbed like a little girl, but he refused to stop. "Be with me, Emmy. Say you'll be with me."

She buried her face in his chest. "How could I say no to you when I've waited for you to say those words to me?"

For the first time in his memory, David's heart was filled with hope. He was pure; washed clean by his love for a woman. He was amazed. They cried and clung to each other throughout the amazing evening that followed. It was the first time David had spent an evening with a woman, without having sex, feeling completely satisfied. David knew he must wait for her; must not dishonor or spoil her. For the very first time he felt like a man. He was a protector, a defender. He would beat back the gates of hell to save her from pain. He had a purpose. He was a new creation.

David got up early the next morning, leaving her lying naked in bed. He moved easily about the kitchen, brewed a fresh pot of coffee, and stirred up blueberry pancake batter. She came down the stairs an hour later in her fuzzy slippers and flannel pajamas and walked into his waiting embrace. When she drew back, he had tucked plane tickets into her pajama bottoms.

"What's this?"

"A ticket to Budapest. I found her, Emmy. Magdalena's mother. She is expecting us. I need your help. We should leave next week."

Emma's face beamed. She nodded excitedly, clutching the tickets in both hands.

Seventeen

Shimon rose early, as he always did, to greet the coming day. It was a crimson dawn. The eastern sky was etched with feathery clouds, sunlight spilling over the horizon in a scarlet bloodbath. Though Shimon was not superstitious, he knew this was not a good sign. Crows circled low over the blonde waters of the Tisza as the sun climbed higher in his bedroom window.

He thanked God for Pieter; the one friend who offered him refuge. The guest room was tiny and spare, with only a clapboard bed, a pillow and quilt, and a bureau for personal items. No matter, he didn't have much, anyway. He snuck out like a thief, late at night, to avoid being seen by prying neighbors, carrying a small satchel with a towel and facecloth, three sets of clothes, a comb, toothbrush and a mirror.

"Come back for the rest once you've found a place of your own."

She was remarkably calm…considering. Several months earlier, word had spread through town about Izabel's second child. Though he tried to dismiss the infant as someone else's bastard, Eva wasn't buying it. He could explain away one illegitimate child, but another was simply more than she could bear.

"You disgust me. I have no love for you anymore, Shimon. I will not humiliate you with a divorce, but you are no longer welcome in this house."

She cried bitterly for many days before declaring the marriage over. She was inconsolable. She would no longer listen to his frail excuses. "You don't understand, Shimon, this is bigger than us."

"Make me understand, then,"

"Understand that I hate you! How could you do this to me? How could you do this to our son?"

"How do you know it's mine, Eva? You know she's been passed around by the men at camp. She has even known her own father! Is this the type of person on whom we should base our marriage?"

Eva came unglued.

"You are a despicable man. You are more than fifteen years older than Izabel, old enough to be her father yourself. How dare you blame a child for her own abuse? You will be cursed by God for your sin and you will bring your curse on your children."

"Children?"

Her face grew pale. Her chin trembled as she clutched a chair to sit down.

"I didn't know. I didn't know. God forgive me, Eva, I didn't know."

"How dare you speak of God to me, Shimon."

Those were her last words to him. She rose up out of the chair and brushed past him to bed, quietly shutting the door behind her so not to wake their son. Shimon stood alone in the darkness.

His marriage was over. He knew this for certain. Neither Eva nor her family would be expected to suffer the disgrace of his ongoing affair with the Rromni. Though the temple elders would tell Eva to honor her wedding vows, they would secretly advise her father to concede to a divorce.

He would be despised, a pariah, tossed aside like a scrap of paper, and she would be forgiven by God, and by men, for the divorce. And he a Halachist! He sighed. He knew he deserved it.

He had misjudged Eva's affection for the girl. He'd assumed she would maintain loyalty to him as when Izabel first became pregnant. But he had gone too far. He took his wife's commitment for granted and, as a result, he lost her forever. He was devastated.

Shimon rose wearily off the bed when he heard the early-morning murmur of Pieter's family. Steeling himself for their playful banter, he shuffled off to the dining room for morning coffee. Pieter's children—Joshua, sixteen, Abraham, fourteen, and Rachel, twelve—were nearly grown, and there was always an argument between them.

Being around the children made Shimon feel strangely disconnected. They were like radiant beams of light shining forth their dueling energies. The house was filled with sound and motion when they were there and, when they left out, the house ached and sighed for their chaotic return. Even the family dog watched for them to spill through the doorway, his rump wagging long before their noise came within earshot. It made his heart sick to be in the periphery of a loving family. He missed his son.

In the dining room, Eva sat patiently waiting for him, one hand resting in her lap, the other cradling a steaming cup of tea. His heart leaped at the sight of her, and then quickly sank when she broke eye contact to continue speaking with Pieter's wife.

"Hello, Shimon."

"Good morning, wife. How are you today?"

"I am feeling well, thank you."

It was so formal between them now. He ached to take her in his arms, but he stood there instead, staring dumbly at her across the table. He held his breath, squeezing the brim of his hat, and waited nervously for instruction. He was small. Timid. Like a child caught stealing cookies.

"Sit down, Shimon," said Pieter's wife. "Eva has come with news of the Rromani camp. She needs your help."

Obediently, he sat down, never taking his eyes off her, as she quietly stirred her tea. They sat in an awkward silence for a minute. Then Pieter cleared his throat to speak. "A battalion of German soldiers camped several miles east along the Romanian border have deployed a squad of reconnaissance troops, and two Arrow-Cross units, to determine the whereabouts of Mártély's Jews."

Pieter's hands trembled. "I received word late last night from a dispatch that the Rromani camp will soon be dismantled. The Germans have abandoned their bivouacs and sentry outposts. They are moving fast. They should arrive at the camp by sundown."

He smacked his fist on the table. "We must move quickly to save ourselves. We will call an immediate assembly of the town elders to determine a course of action. We must protect our people from the bastards. They will surely kill every Jew in this village. We cannot sit here and wait to be slaughtered. If we cannot defend ourselves, we should flee."

"Where will we run to," asked Shimon. "You think the Germans haven't anticipated this? They are not stupid. The gentiles won't help us. The churches have given them an accounting of our whereabouts. The Reich has swept across Eastern Europe like a plague of locusts. There is nowhere for us to hide."

Pieter's wife began to sob. "Our sons are in the resistance. The Germans will be looking for them. They say we should stay and fight, not hide away like mice in the attic walls. They say we must distribute arms to the men to use for our defense. They are the ones who sounded the alarm last night."

Pieter silenced her. "We have a small cache of weapons hidden in the attic. We can fight. But what match are we against automatic weapons and artillery? I say we send the older boys ahead to make a way for the women and children. It's our only hope of survival."

Shimon shook his head vehemently. "No. We should stay. We are a tiny village. Why would the Nazis be concerned with a ragtag group of Jews in a remote region of Csongrád? We are insignificant. Besides, what chance would my family have of surviving the journey? Where would we go? We would be caught and executed."

"I must send my sons away or they will be shot like dogs in the street," Pieter cried.

Shimon stroked his beard thoughtfully. "Whoever chooses to, is free to go. Each man must make that choice for himself and his family. This is my home and I don't intend to leave it. I will not scurry into the hills like a rat. We stay."

Shimon and Eva watched Pieter and his wife walk their sons outside. The father brusquely handed a large satchel of bread, cheese and dried fruit to the oldest boy, saying, "Whatever you hear, do not turn back. It is no longer safe here."

The children wept openly, clinging to their mother.

"Take the river south to safe passage. Trust no one. Stay off the main roads. Stay hidden. God be with you, my sons."

Pieter's wife and daughter clung together, sobbing, as they watched the teenagers hurry for the nearby trees. What could Shimon do? His son was too young to be separated from his mother, and she was with child. He cursed himself; he was certain she could have made the journey if she were not pregnant.

He turned to look at his pregnant wife, desperate to protect her. He could not falter. God demanded that he meet his destiny with courage. As every man should. "I swear to God I will let no harm come to this family. I demand that you return home immediately, wife."

"And what of Izabel, Shimon? You heard Pieter. They will be slaughtered. Are you at peace with sitting idle, while Izabel and your daughter are murdered? Will you be a coward before the eyes of our God? Even now as you meet your own end?"

Shimon regarded her with cold indifference.

"I will take care of my own. God willing. Now, go home, Eva; bring our son back here."

Eva glared at him, teary-eyed, then ran for home.

As the remaining family prayed over supper, there came a brisk knock at the door. The old man finished his prayer, glanced at Shimon, then moved to the door. Before he could answer, the door was pushed open, and a small group of gendarmes moved inside. The men leered at Rachel until one scar-faced, dark-skinned Romanian asked if he was Pieter Loucks.

"I am Rabbi Loucks."

The men clapped each other on the back, speaking coarsely in a harsh Romanian dialect.

"Rabbi, we ask you to organize a committee of leaders to meet the Germans at temple this night. Do you know the whereabouts of Shimon Szótemel?"

Pieter didn't bat an eye. "No, sir, I do not. He is on holiday at his wife's home in Villány. I have not seen him this past month."

The foul-smelling man glowered across the room at Shimon.

Pieter attempted to satisfy the obvious question. "This is my nephew Saul. From Pest."

Shimon rose to his feet. The dark man studied him. Shimon licked his lips nervously. *If he asks for identification, I'm a dead man standing here!*

Shimon opened his mouth to speak when the dark man barked, "I expect to see both of you at the temple after we finish cleaning out that Gypsy shit-hole. Gather your leaders to the temple. The Germans wish to discuss the Jewish relocation. The dark man tipped his hat to Pieter's wife, staring down Rachel's blouse, then suddenly walked out, slamming the door behind him.

"Thank God. Thank God." Pieter fell to his knees and wept. "God help the poor souls in that camp. God protect and watch over us. Deliver us from this evil."

"I must go." Shimon's voice cracked with fear—and rage.

"I need you here, Shimon. We must plan our negotiation." Shimon saw a weird light in his friend's eyes.

"Start without me, Pieter. I need to gather my family. They are not safe alone. I'll be back."

Shimon's stomach crawled into his throat, filling his mouth with bile. Where was she? The phony documents he bought were still at the house. A contact in Budapest had introduced him to a policeman who moonlighted as a forger. The man was a professional, worth the money, and the risk. All the preparations were made. They'd even packed a small knapsack for each of them with clothing, food and water. Had Eva left without him?

Ten minutes later, Shimon burst through the front door of his home, breathless and pale.

"My Lord, Shimon, you scared me half to death!" Eva's mother sat on the sofa, reading a book.

"Where is she?"

"Who?"

"For God's sake. Eva…my wife!"

His mother-in-law glared at him over the top of her book. The look was eerily reminiscent of the one Eva had given him a few hours earlier. She sighed wearily, slid her glasses down the bridge of her nose, and then closed her book.

"*Where is she?*"

Sarai covered her mouth with her hands. Her eyes opened wide in alarm.

"She's gone, Shimon. She said she had to see Izabel. She's left David asleep on the bed. Please don't wake him, he's resting so peacefully."

Shimon tore for the bedroom door. He wrenched it open.

What have you done, Eva?

Sarai cried aloud behind him. "The baby was here. She must have taken him with her, Shimon. I swear, I didn't know. What is happening?"

Shimon ignored her, slamming open the closet door and pushing aside the clothing. Behind the clothes, he began to feel along the wall for a loose board. He pried it open with trembling fingers.

It's gone. My God, it's gone. What have you done, wife? He tore out his disheveled hair, yelling into the empty hiding space. It stared coolly back at him.

"What is it? What's wrong, Shimon?"

"Mother, you must go to Pieter's home right now. Leave everything and go. *Go now!*"

"Yes. Yes. All right, son, I'm going."

"We will be right behind you, Sarai. I need to find your daughter first."

"You're scaring me, Shimon. I will go, but you must promise me you'll find her. I beg you." She paused. "She's carrying your child, Shimon. Dear God in heaven, protect my daughter. Damn that Gypsy."

"*Go!*"

The old woman grabbed her grandson's knapsack and pounded out the door in the direction of Pieter's house. Shimon paused at the bedroom door to take one last look at the remaining knapsack on the bed. He blinked back tears and followed his mother-in-law out the door without bothering to lock it behind him.

Shimon headed north towards the river. The sky was overcast; the air thick and still. Or was that his imagination? Flocks of egrets eyed him nervously from the surrounding marshes.

The birds stepped gingerly with reed-like legs over sinking patches of scrub, when a sudden alarm call sent them into frenzied flight. They pirouetted and swayed low over the tree line, then settled back down amidst the muddy marsh grass and rustling cattails.

Shimon walked deeper into the woods that surrounded the Tisza. Beady, red eyes reflected the receding light in an overhead tree branch. A mother opossum issued an ominous hiss at Shimon as her babies clung to her and stared.

Not much further now.

In the distance, Shimon heard automatic gunfire in the direction of the camp. He hesitated. Should he continue north to Izabel's makeshift home, or turn south towards the camp?

Where are you, wife?

His hands shook as he stopped to roll a cigarette. He inhaled long drags of smoke into his lungs, listening to the sound of shots ringing out, and the angry shouting of men. He swallowed hard. He turned north towards safety.

Shimon stopped short when he heard a baby crying in the distance. He spat on the ground, stubbed out his cigarette, then headed south toward the distant lights.

No turning back now. You will see, my darling. I am no coward.

The trees thinned a short distance from the clearing. Shimon moved forward to take refuge behind an oak, and then watched as troops flushed the women and children from their hiding places, out onto the open floodplain. Some fired pistols into tents and wagons, cursing loudly in German; others waved service rifles high in the air, firing even more rounds overhead. A hail of bullets rained down on the crowd. One grazed the skin of Shimon's forearm, burning a welt into his flesh. He fell hard against the tree, using his fist to stifle a scream of pain.

The group of miscreants from Pieter's house watched as German soldiers slowly moved the frightened families into a nearby bog. Occasionally, someone rushed wildly for the tree line, but the footing was soft, and they were targeted by a swinging rifle. The Gypsies huddled together in a wide circle as the goon squad encircled them, herding them together like a pack of hunting dogs before taking the weakest deer.

Screams exploded from a tent on the south end of camp. His stomach heaved as he watched an Arrow-Cross guard pull an old woman out of the tent by her hair. He threw her down on the ground as she begged him for mercy. The Romanian cursed bitterly, complaining she'd hidden her children inside a trunk. Cruel laughter rang out at her desperation.

Shimon felt his knees weaken when he recognized her. It was Izabel's mother. The Germans sneered at her as she lay on the ground at their feet, while the Arrow-Cross guards dragged her screaming children outside one at a time.

Shimon's mouth twitched as he watched her beg for her children's lives. Snot dripped over the mud-caked boots that she kissed in earnest. The dark Romanian took hold of her oldest child, threw him onto the ground, and shot him in the back with a Russian Mosin-Nagant rifle. The boy tried to crawl away on his belly, but the man fired twice more. Agonized wails rose from the entire camp; the howling of Iza's mother plain above the din.

Shimon fell to his knees and watched as Romanian guards murdered her five remaining children. An enraged soldier stomped on the youngest, an 18-month-old baby, her neck snapping audibly beneath his feet.

The Rroma were hysterical. The women clutched their babies to their breasts as the men tried to break through the line. Immediately, the Germans opened fire on them with their MP40's in a hail of bullets.

Shimon stumbled to his feet and ran into the clearing. The old Rromani woman sat on the ground, her infant's life draining away in her blood-soaked dress. She rocked back and forth, her mouth open wide in a death yaw, the silent scream of the insane.

"Come on," Shimon ordered. "Come on!"

He tugged violently on her arm. Her eyes were open wide. Expressionless. Her lower jaw hung slack and drool seeped from the corner of her mouth. She was oblivious;

her mind gone. He struck her in the face as the soldiers picked off the remaining Rroma.

Shimon glanced at the bog and saw only two or three children left standing. They were crying inconsolably, wading through the bodies, searching for their parents. He heard the muffled cries of infants trapped beneath their dying mothers. A German kicked one young mother's body aside to fire a bullet into her squalling infant. Shimon heard another soldier yell, "Don't waste your bullets. They'll be dead by sundown."

All was quiet except for the lonely crying of a baby trailing up from the bog. Izabel's mother lay motionless on the ground. Shimon stood up and began walking towards the sound. He was mesmerized. A soldier saw him coming and ordered him to lie on the ground. Shimon kept walking.

That is my son! זְגִירְשְׁעַג גְוּאָלְד *For heaven's sake!*

His feet moved slowly—mechanically. The dark Romanian walked up to him and pointed a Lüger at Shimon's face.

"Lie down, you stupid Jew!"

"What's wrong with him? Is he deaf?"

Shimon searched the ground, shuffling off in the direction of the haunting sound. The cries were growing weaker, trailing off into silence. Shimon searched back and forth over the bloody ground, his salty tears cascading down over the moist earth.

He spoke in Hebrew, "Can you hear him crying? Where is he? Where is my son?"

The soldier raised his gun to eye level.

"Where is he?"

"In hell." He fired a single bullet into Shimon's spine. Shimon crumbled to the ground. He felt the blood rushing from the gaping wound. He gurgled. Blood spattered from his lips.

"Eva."

"What did the Jew say?"

"Does it matter?"

He fired another round into his brain.

Eighteen

"May I hold her?"

Izabel looked warily up at Eva from her seat on the hard-packed dirt floor, while Magdalena and David played in a distant corner of the shack. Magda yelped indignantly when David tore one of her paper dolls in two, his fat fingers ripping through her cherished treasure-box.

"Mama?"

"Let him play, Magdalena. For shame, a big girl like you! He is your brother."

Izabel sighed wearily, plucking the infant from her swollen breast.

"I'm sorry for the mess, Eva. I was not expecting anyone today."

She expertly wrapped her infant in a swaddling cloth, handing her unceremoniously to Eva.

"I'm glad you're here, Eva, I wanted you to hear this from my lips. I'm sorry. I was wrong to have hurt you. It's over between Shimon and me; I've not spoken to him in many months. I would do anything to spare you more pain. Tell me what I can do?"

"Let me hold her, Izabel."

"She's yours if you want her. Isn't she lovely with her green eyes and red lips? She will be my great beauty."

"Just like her mother," Eva murmured.

"Take her, Eva, she's yours. I would give you both children if it would make things right between us. They are my heart, given to you freely. You're the only woman that ever loved me; ever believed in me. Everything that I have in this world belongs to you. I don't want to live knowing that you hate me. I couldn't bear it."

Stunned by her emotional confession, Eva squeezed the soft cocoon that encased Izabel's infant daughter. She was relived to hear her words. She knew Iza had cut all ties to Shimon, but she didn't know the affair had produced a second child.

Damn him! He's ruined her life.

She should hate Izabel for her part in their betrayal, but the truth was she felt even more connected to the girl. They were forever tied by blood, by passion, and history. Shimon's moral weakness had wrung out the skinny, little Rromani girl with the tired eyes and the persistent cough, but maybe she could make things right by securing a future for her and her daughters. If only she were willing to return the favor.

Eva cuddled the baby near her face, breathing in the warm, clean scent. She was already stunning. She had the same exotic features of her Rromani mother, but without the dark mahogany skin. She had a thick shock of wavy, amber-colored hair, which Izabel had lovingly pulled away from her face with a jeweled straight pin. Magdalena was also scrubbed pink, her black curls cascading down her back from out of a patch of dark blue ribbons.

"You're a good mother, Izabel. I knew you would be. Your daughters are exquisite. How blessed you are."

"They are healthy and strong. I'm thankful to God, for it won't be an easy life. They will always be different. Oh, Eva, I don't know what I'll do! I know in my heart we can't stay here. I must take them far away. But how?"

Izabel's slender thin frame trembled beneath her flowing skirts.

She's so young...just a child herself. It will be to her advantage.

She wasn't the same coquettish girl Eva first met three years earlier. She was a woman now. Eva was sad for her. For her lost innocence, for her family history, for her isolation. Such losses were incomprehensible to Eva. She had always been cared for. Loved and cherished. How would it feel to be left in solitude with two small children in the heart of the wilderness?

"Have you eaten, Iza? You look a little pale."

"No. Mama is bringing supper. She is late, though. I am a bit hungry."

"Let's take a meal together. I have something to ask you."

"All I can offer you is hot tea and galúshki."

"What's that?"

"Sweet almond dumplings."

"That sounds lovely."

The two girls prepared an early supper, chattering on like old friends. Izabel sat cross-legged on the floor and poured a cup of tea for each of them. Looking over the top of her cup, she said shyly, "I've missed you. You mean the world to me."

Eva sat on the floor across from her friend, and played with the silky curls on the baby's forehead. "I'm glad. We are truly sisters; forever bound by love. I must carry the burden of not seeing my husband's deceit. I should have known. I should have stopped it. You don't understand now, Iza, you are just a child, and I love my husband, but what Shimon did to you was wrong. He ruined your chance for a better life. I expected great things from you. And all the while, my husband was imposing his great will and sinful desire on you...a child. It sickens me."

Iza's face darkened.

"I am not a child, Eva. In my culture, I am a woman now. I'm a mother."

"How old are you, Izabel?"

"Nearly seventeen!"

"Yes, you are a woman, Iza. I'm sorry, little sister. I did not mean to offend." Eva smiled.

"It is my sin to bear, Eva. Men have brute strength, the power of sinew and bone, but it's women who hold sway. For by a woman's gentle touch, with her soft voice, in her sensuous curves, she controls the man. You are beautiful, Eva, you know of what I speak. Women born of great beauty possess great power. They need only a smile to get their way. Do not blame your husband, Eva, he is just a man. I was a fool to believe in him."

"Believe in him?"

"That he would take care of me. Mama was right all along. All I ever wanted was to be loved, Eva. My mistake was in my blindness to the love you offered me as a sister. My blindness was in mistaking his passion for love." She started to cry. "How could I be so stupid?"

"Don't cry, Iza. The children will hear."

"What will I do? How will we survive?"

"You will survive, Izabel. You are a survivor. I am here to offer my help, if you will help me in return…"

Iza looked at her eagerly.

"You must leave here. You must leave now. German soldiers will be at the Rromani camp by midday. Izabel, they will murder every Gypsy, and every Jew, in Mártély. You must flee for your children's lives."

"What are you saying?"

"They're merciless, sister. They've already decimated entire villages in Romania."

"I know of these men, Eva. These German Nazis. They are very dangerous. I have to warn my family."

"No, Iza. You must flee south. God will deliver the faithful. You must run!"

"But where? How?"

"I have birth certificates and passports. You can claim to have lost Magdalena's papers along the way. You will use these documents in my place and you will take David with you."

Izabel stared at her, her mouth open wide.

"Please don't say no. You are my only hope for David. He is a Jew. He will be put to death if caught. We are all being hunted, Jews and Gypsies, we are all the same now. Death is the great equalizer. You cannot refuse me, Iza! I won't accept it."

Iza balked.

"I am offering to save your life, despite your betrayal of me, in exchange for the life of my son. I don't want your children, Izabel; I want you to take mine. I know that you love me. I know you will be a good mother to David. I know you'll spend the rest of your days in service to him out of love for me. Make your amends, Iza. Save my son's life."

"Where will we go?"

"Shimon and I have secured safe passage to the town of Djála. You must travel thirty miles south along the Tisza to the place where the river forks in two. Take the branch that splits southwest, to the border of Juguslavija."

A suspicious rustling interrupted her. After a brief silence, Eva continued.

"There is a farmhouse several miles west of Djála. A Christian family is expecting you. They are good people, descendants of Bulgarian sheep herders, and family friends for many generations. They will give you food and shelter and provide transportation overland to Varna, on the east coast of Bulgaria. Apply for an America visa as soon as you arrive."

Izabel gave her a doubtful look as her hand reached out to touch her child.

"You will be in great peril on this journey. Make haste to the farm, for Arrow-Cross guards will be looking for stragglers, and the townspeople will betray you if you're sighted. Travel only at night. Ration the food I've packed for the journey."

"Don't worry, sister. I am as silent as the fog. But I've never moved with such small children."

"I believe in you, Iza. I know you can make it. You are the bravest girl I know."

"I am afraid. What if I don't make it?"

"Then we'll be together in the after-life. You are the best hope for my family's survival. Have courage. Be smart. And survive."

"But what of you?"

"I am very sick with Shimon's child. I cannot travel. I would slow you down."

"I won't leave you!"

"You must. I will forestall any efforts to search for you. Now change out of your skirts, they draw too much attention. Here are a pair of Shimon's pants for you to stay warm. Get dressed. Time is wasting."

They heard shots ring out in the direction of the camp. Iza moaned, "Mama!"

"They are sooner than I expected. Hurry! Dress Magda in many layers."

When Izabel snatched the girl away from her toys, she immediately began to wail. Right on cue, David began to cry, standing next to his sister.

"Hush," Iza snapped. "I don't want to hear another sound, Magda, or I swear I will strike you! Be silent."

The little girl looked at her mother and sniffed.

Eva pulled her son into her arms and kissed him on his face. Though the boy squirmed to run back to his play, she held firm, whispering in his ear.

"You will live. You will be happy."

She set David down on the floor next to his sister, and clapped her hands to get their attention.

"You will listen to Izabel and do what you're told. Be quiet when you're told. Lie down when you're told and sleep when you're told. If you are good children, I will bring you both special presents."

"A surprise?"

"Yes!"

"I want a doll! I want a dress!"

"I want Papa," sniffed David.

Eva knelt down in front of her son and cradled him in her arms.

"Izabel is your mother now. You must mind her until your father and I come for you. Then we will bring your surprise. What would you like, David?"

Softly, he said, "A toy train? With a red caboose."

"You will have them, I promise. I love you, David."

She helped Izabel tie her infant onto her chest in a makeshift harness made of strips of torn skirt. They covered the baby beneath several woolen shirts to protect her from the night air. They left the primitive cabin and walked out to the open path. Iza clicked her tongue at the children, walking ahead of her on the dirt path, hand in hand. She whirled around to hug her friend.

Eva returned her hug. "You have what you need. Here are the documents, some money, and a letter of introduction to our friends. Don't be afraid, Iza. I will pray for you."

"And I you, sister. Don't be far behind."

Eva held her tears as she watched her only son racing down the path, a tiny hand in Iza's grasp, his chubby legs trotting to keep pace. Iza bent down to say something to him. Eva could barely see the glimpse of a smile as they walked out of sight. She fought the overwhelming urge to collapse on the ground and sob, or chase him down the path, for she knew her interference would seal his fate.

She stood outside the cabin, watching the ghostly image of her son being led away, innocent to the shadow that obscured his future.

I've left his fate in the hands of another. Have I done the right thing, Lord? Have I failed my only son?

She prayed to God for His mercy, for His protection, for safe passage, gladly offering her own life in trade. Eva heard the crack of a gun in the distance and she broke for home. She ran through the trees, branches snapping against her body, and sobbed great, heaving sobs. The cacophony of automatic gunfire chased her, followed by a blaze of fire that licked upwards, beautiful against the emerging twilight stars.

She ran, and ran, and ran. She wished she could run all the way to the Mediterranean Sea and sail away on a great masted ship to some distant land. She ran until the air burned in her lungs and her legs twitched violently beneath her. It felt good to run. It was something, at least. She was alive. And she would not meet her death quietly, for she carried another inside her. It moved, it was still alive, she could feel it.

Eva wiped her blearied face as she entered the town, refreshed, renewed, resolved to keep her family together. She loved her husband. Her heart was filled with hope as she burst into Pieter's house, searching frantically for him.

"Shimon! Shimon," she called out. She tore about the house, but the house stood silent, refusing to give up its secrets. Eva heard a rustling noise behind her. She wheeled about and saw the family dog lying dead behind the door, a uniformed Arrow-Cross guard beside it.

"Who are you? Where's the family that lives here?"

"Who are you," asked the dark Romanian. He stroked his wiry moustache, studying her.

Eva stood her ground, staring defiantly at his ugly, pockmarked face. His uniform reeked. It filled the room with the smell of sweat, and something else. She caught the faint odor of burnt hair in his clothing. He was rank with the smell of death.

"How dare you enter this house," she hissed. Get out!"

He laughed at her brazenness, and moved close to touch her hair.

"Are you a Jew?"

"Are you a Christian?"

His eyes grew black at the challenge. He cupped a hand around her slender neck.

"Are you a Jew?"

"Yes, I'm a Jew. What do you call yourself?"

He squeezed until her windpipe popped. Eva's face turned blue and her eyes bulged from their sockets. She didn't struggle. She stared into the dark man's eyes, waiting for the blackness to engulf her. Suddenly, he released his grip, and she fell to the floor, gasping for air.

I am not afraid of you. My son lives, therefore, I too live.

"Bitch," he spat. "Get outside with the others. Move! Before I shoot you here."

He watched her stumble out the door, and then he sat down to eat a biscuit left on the supper table. Eva ran into the street. Arrow-Cross Guards invaded and cleared houses, moving Mártély's Jews into a wooded area beside the Temple Harzion. Eva lurched down the street, pushed forward by marauding soldiers. When she passed by her Catholic neighbor's house, she raised a hand at the pulled-back front curtains, then watched as they fell back into place.

Mártély's Jews milled about next to the temple, resting on trunks and suitcases. Eva cried out at the sight of Pieter's family. His wife embraced her, kissing her face.

"Thank God, Eva. We thought you'd never come. Where is Shimon?"

"I thought he was with you?"

Pieter glanced at his wife, then grabbed Eva in a great bear hug.

"Never mind girl, Shimon can take care of himself."

"Where is David?" Eva's mother cried.

"I let him go."

"Go? Go where?"

"He's safe, mama, don't worry."

"Don't worry? How can you tell me not to worry? What did you do with him? Don't tell me you left him with that girl?"

Eva looked away.

"How could you? You fool!"

"Be quiet, mama. I can take care of my own son."

"Shimon is out looking for you. You've brought death on your husband because of your foolish affection for that girl. God forgive you."

"Shut up, both of you," Pieter's wife said. "What's done is done!"

A German officer approached the group, smiling. He offered his hand to Pieter. Pieter took it hesitantly.

"What a pleasure to finally meet a true Rabbi. I have much I'd like to discuss with you, but I must commence with the business at hand. Have you called a group of your leaders to speak on behalf of the community?"

"I have."

"Shall we go inside the temple, as an act of good faith, to discuss the terms of the relocation?"

Pieter eyed him suspiciously for a moment, then gathered the men to him. They were young men and old men, farmers and merchants and doctors and university students, husbands and bachelors. The best and brightest that Mártély had to offer, all marched, single-file, into the temple; led like lambs to slaughter by their beloved Rabbi. When the last man entered the temple, the field commander ordered the temple doors closed.

The rabbi raised a hand in protest. "Wait."

But the German's kept him from entering, asking him to stand fast for a moment. Pieter stood, obediently waiting, when the Arrow-Cross guards slammed the temple doors behind him. Suddenly, the Germans nailed the doors shut, hammering fast, as the men inside pounded furiously on the doors. The field commander stood firm, hands on his hips, as he shouted at the remaining women and children.

"Let this be an example of what will happen to anyone who dares challenge me. We know this town is abetting political dissidents who have harassed my men like sand fleas. We know that Mártély harbors several members of a Jewish resistance. We don't believe the men inside your temple are involved. Maybe they are, maybe they aren't. Maybe they're innocent like the three German soldiers that were killed in a raid on our camp two weeks ago."

"I will give Mártély's Jews one chance to redeem themselves before we set fire to the temple. Turn over the resistors, and your men will live; refuse, and they die."

Pieter stood before the temple door with tears streaming down his cheeks, eyes pleading to the friends and neighbors looking at him. The crowd was agitated, on the verge of hysterics. Some prayed, some cried, others argued or swore. But no one spoke against the Rabbi's sons.

"Give me names!"

The remaining men glared defiantly at the Germans, as the women wrung their hands and moaned.

"Their blood will be on your heads!"

An old man shouted, "They are not here. They have gone. Leave us in peace."

"Where did they go?"

The old man mumbled, dropping his head. A soldier dragged him out, kicking and swearing, and threw him at the feet of the German officer.

"I want names," he whispered.

The Rabbi wrung his hands, pleading in Hebrew, imploring the man's silence.

"Shut your devil's tongue." He smashed Pieter in the mouth, knocking him to the ground.

"You are a whore," the old man cursed in Hebrew. The German unholstered his Lűger, firing two rounds into the man's skull.

Fury on the officer's face—he screamed. "Light it up!"

Soldiers rushed forward, dragging gasoline cans from their vehicles, spraying the wooden structure until it reeked. The Jews inside the temple trampled on furniture, smashing glass out of windows, and shrieked for help, as their families stood helpless a few feet away.

One woman raced to an east window to help her husband climb out. Two Arrow-Cross soldiers immediately gunned her down before her husband's eyes. He wailed out the broken glass when a rifle round caught him in his left cheek. His eyes flew open in surprise, when a second round sheared off the top third of his head. He collapsed straight down, like a house of cards, or a marionette that had lost a string.

"Burn it down, burn it down, burn it down," screamed the officer to his men.

The dark guard tossed an incendiary grenade through the shattered window, igniting the building like a matchstick. Eva stood frozen amidst a sea of bleating lambs, their bodies pressing in close, shrieks and cries swirling about her like some freakish orchestral movement. She watched as the men beat on the doors and walls of the temple, screaming for help, crying out to God to save them. She heard one man beg for death before the flames consumed him. Mártély's Jews were on the verge of a riot when the soldiers began sweeping the crowd with gunfire.

"Move out," they screamed.

They slowly drove the crowd south to the road, and the train yards, of Szégéd. Shots rang over her head as the panicked people ran from the burning temple towards an uncertain fate.

The screaming from within reached a fever pitch as the people were consumed by flames. She saw Mártély's town doctor beating flames off of himself, screaming like a wounded animal, his face twisted with pain. For a moment, their eyes locked through the glass, then he threw himself out through the west window. He was met with dozens of MP30 rounds, riddling holes into his charred flesh. Eva bent forward to vomit on the ground. The physician dangled from the window, his upper-torso bleeding and bare, though he continued to burn from the waist down.

"Ugh."

A young soldier gagged involuntarily as he used his service rifle to shove the body back inside to be engulfed in the inferno.

"Move on!"

The field commander shouted over the noise of the building as it began to collapse.

"You. Come here."

The dark guard motioned to her to follow him into a strand of trees. There, she saw twelve-year-old Rachel on the ground, two soldiers standing watch, while a third humped her furiously. Eva screamed, enraged, attracting the attention of the officer. He ran at the men, cursing loudly in German, and the two soldiers sprinted off through the trees. The Commander came up behind the Romanian guard raping the girl on the ground, and shot him in the back as he continued to thrust inside her.

"Fucking animal."

When the officer kicked off the guard, Eva saw the bullet had gone clean through, ripping a quarter-inch sized hole into the girl's chest. Air sucked out of the wound as she struggled to breathe. Eva fought to reach her in her final moments, but the commander turned to look at them, saying they'd better move on, or they'd be next. The dark man shoved her out ahead of him, shrugging at the German officer.

She turned to take one last look at Rachel. The girl lay on the ground, her eyes open wide, mouth agape as if to speak. Rachel was the lucky one. She was beyond the madness now, having yielded to a merciful death. A short distance from where the girl lay, Pieter's wife ran toward her, calling to her dead daughter.

"Rachel! Rachel! Rachel!"

"Eva, have you seen Rachel? I've lost her. She must have run off."

"No," she lied, "I haven't seen her. She's a smart girl. She'll hide away until they've gone, then she'll go find her brothers. Don't worry, she's a smart one, that girl. Let her go, Mama. She's better here."

"Yes," the woman said miserably. "You are right. I must trust that God will protect my children. We must have faith now."

Eva gave her a haggard smile. "Yes. What else have we?"

Nineteen

Izabel was first to the river. She padded down with bare feet, loosening her clothes as she walked. When she reached the shoreline, she kneeled at the water's edge to dip a soiled rag into the current, wringing out the cool water with both hands. Her legs trembled with fatigue; her back ached with muscle spasms. She rubbed at her dirt crusted face and neck, scrubbing under her arms, and between her legs. The chilly water was refreshing.

She yearned to lie down next to the cool waters on her back, and stare up at the stars, and listen to the bickering of the birds overhead, and smell the fragrant winds that blew through the sweet pines; an aromatic blend of pine needles, wet earth, damp sand and wild crocuses.

A small, white butterfly drew her attention as it fluttered erratically over the sand, its sugar wings glistening in the early morning air. The creature perched atop a shrub. It moved its wings, open and closed, waiting for the sun to dry the dew, waiting to fly across the desolate plains of the Alföld. How she yearned to be little again, moving from town to town, running next to the caravan, exploring the woods and streams and open spaces.

Izabel was used to the hard life and constant struggle of Gypsies. Though Rroma were shunned by the local residents of every new village and town, they themselves comprised a tight-knit community. They shared resources. They lived together. They ate together. They arranged marriages. They brought children into the world. They buried their dead.

Izabel reflected that over the centuries, no matter what pressures threatened from the outside world, the travelers remained united. There was strength in numbers. Rroma had proven themselves hardy and pragmatic, opportunists in a world governed by the non-Rroma, or *gadže*. They eked out an existence in the periphery of the modern world; present but unaccounted for.

Throughout Hungary, Rromani men quietly worked collecting gold deposits from the river bottoms. In Western Europe, they worked as blade sharpeners. Barely noticed by passersby, they sharpened scissors and knives with portable whetstone wheels on busy street corners. They were horse traders, fortune tellers and metal workers.

Izabel's eyes began to fill with tears. They were also husbands, mothers, children and grandparents. Family remained the central focus in Rromani society. Rromani culture was simple yet effective: A loyalty to family, a belief in God and the devil, a belief in predestiny, adherence to Rromanija standards and an ability to adapt to change.

Izabel knew that their unwillingness to assimilate with non-Rroma came from their innate fear of polluting themselves by association with those who were unclean.

This isolation led to widespread persecution which, though not historically documented by Rroma, the telling was evident in a rich, oral history.

They had no political or military strength, no geographical territory to claim as a homeland, no identifiable history, religion or language. They were the perfect victims: powerless, faceless, voiceless and worthless. Their abuse only led to strengthen their bonds of kinship. And they survived.

The simple fact of her physical separation from her family made Izabel's journey more perilous, and their survival less likely, with each passing day. Iza had abandoned Rromani rules of cleanliness soon after walking into the wilderness with her children. The rules were complex.

Izabel, like the rest of her people, believed in one God, *o Devel*, and the devil, *o Beng*, and they believed there was a constant struggle between them for dominance over Rroma lives. From her mother she learned that to live properly meant abiding by a set of behaviors to maintain spiritual balance. The Rromani people shared a dualistic perspective of the universe, and notions of ritual pollution, central to Rromani belief, were prevalent. Contact between the mouth and various utensils shared with others at a meal were avoided to eliminate risk of contamination. The surest way to avoid risk of contamination was to eat with the fingers.

Her mother, Greta Remény, taught her well. Rroma also divided foods into "ordinary" and "lucky" categories. This division reflected the close relationship between food and health, as particular ingredients were not only beneficial to the physical self, but also to the spiritual. Rroma did not prepare dishes far in advance of their being eaten and did not keep any leftover food.

Izabel remembered her mother whispering special cautions to her. A woman must not be seen with her legs uncovered. This was considered a grave offense. The clothing of men and woman would never be washed together. Separate pails would be used for the different uses of water. A menstruating girl, or pregnant woman, was considered ritually unclean throughout her entire condition. Even the horses had to take water upstream from where a pregnant woman was allowed to wash.

Izabel sighed as the sun washed her aching muscles. That was all a distant memory now. She was making up her own rules as she went. She missed the comfort found in the Rromanija. But such restrictions would not assure their survival out here in the wild. If God let her live, she would be accountable for her infractions.

She could not think about it. She would just stay here and rest for awhile. Just for awhile.

All too soon she heard the distant crying of an infant. She tried to ignore it, but the sound began to penetrate the pre-dawn silence. She glanced over her shoulder toward the noise, and continued to drink from a fresh pool of rainwater. A thin wail rose up over the tree line. She flecked a few more beads of moisture onto her forehead and quickly refastened her clothing.

She moved quickly into the dense underbrush, puffing up to scold her oldest daughter for letting her sister cry aloud. She came to the place beneath the lilac bush where she left the children, and saw Magdalena desperately rocking Jael in her skinny arms, humming aloud in a wavering voice.

"Shush, shush," Magdalena scolded.

Izabel was startled to recognize the same tone and inflection she herself had used with her own siblings only a few years earlier. Her heart suddenly filled with pity for the girl, for a future still clouded by shadow and uncertainty. Magdalena had a glazed-over expression and black circles that curled around her eye sockets. David lay on the ground at his half-sister's feet.

"Let your brother sleep. Come take a bath."

"She won't stop crying, mama," she complained. "I tried to keep her quiet. I don't think she likes me."

"She likes you just fine, daughter."

She swept up the infant and secured her in a bundle against her sharply protruding ribcage. "How could she not like you, goose? You are her big sister."

She glanced over at her daughter.

She is too thin. We are all starving. They suffer great hunger, yet this one never complains.

"Mama?"

"Come, girl, let's get you clean!"

She winced as she felt the baby latch onto a breast. They moved carefully to the water, Iza walking ahead of her daughter. She quickly stripped Magda bare and walked her into the slow-moving current. She washed her quickly to prevent a chill, rubbing her skin with a smooth stone to scour away the soot.

Iza was constantly amazed at how much grime built up on the children's bodies—they were like magnets for the dirt. She scrubbed Magdalena until her skin shone.

"I will wash your hair when we arrive. The oil will protect against head lice."

Iza started moving Magda onto the shore when the girl let out a horrified scream. Iza lifted her hand to silence her, and heard David's sleepy voice coming out of the trees.

"You left me," the voice accused. "I thought you all left me." His tiny voiced quaked in the shadows.

"David," she said sharply. "You do *not* come down to the river alone. You do *not* move an inch unless you are told. And you do *not* present yourself when women are bathing! This is inappropriate. Go back at once."

He began to wail. Iza felt the blood rushing in her ears. She clenched her fists at her sides. She breathed deeply, trying to calm her rage, as she watched the boy step into the clearing, staggering towards them, his face puffy and tear-stained.

"I want mama," he cried. "I want to go home."

Iza stood hating him.

Ungrateful brat! We would not be here, starving, if it weren't for you.

The past few days had been excruciating. They had managed to move out of Mártély at a steady clip, walking about five miles that first day. But by the next, David had become uncooperative and emotional. He begged to return to his mother, again and again, until his wailing rang out like a great clarion call across the water. He threw tremendous tantrums, refusing to move, refusing to eat, until threatened with a beating. They moved about only at night and then, instead of sleeping, spent the days assuaging a hysterical three-year-old.

Now, several days into the journey, David walked zombie-like behind his sister. He marched on stilted legs, head dragging, tired eyes staring at the ground. Magdalena's bright eyes darted back and forth across the landscape, calling to her brother in a singsong voice when she discovered a wild berry bush or a black plum thicket. Iza knew the fruit would give them loose stools, but she hadn't the heart to scold them. She was grateful for the tiny moments of joy, hopeful they would boost the children's spirits.

Iza stared at the boy who screamed at her from across the river. He was nearly three, but no bigger than an eighteen-month old. Sudden, dramatic weight loss had given an odd look to his face. His cheeks and eyes were sunken; his forehead crisscrossed with blue veins. His clothes draped over his skeletal frame, his hands and feet disproportionately large at the end of stick limbs.

Fighting the urge to break him in half, Iza told her daughter to move to the shallows upstream to fish, so she could bathe David.

"We will risk a small fire today."

The girl stared at her mother apprehensively for a moment, and then skipped off to retrieve the knapsack that held their fishing line and steel hooks.

"If I can capture a dragonfly, Mama, I'll use it to bring you a giant fish."

Iza watched her flit out of sight. She then turned her attention to the child still standing on the opposite shore. He sucked his thumb and sniffled as he watched his sister run to play. When Magdalena had passed out of his sight, Iza heard him begin to tune up again.

"Come here, baby."

He stared at her distrustfully, his knees trembling with exhaustion.

"Come here, David. I won't hurt you. Let me wash you clean."

He remained unmoved. She softened her voice.

"My poor baby. Don't be afraid. I am your mother now. I won't ever hurt you."

Her gentle words sent him sailing into the chilly waters to her, his tiny white teeth forcing a smile as he approached her.

"Come here, child."

She gently lifted his shirt to bathe him, and gasped in shock at his condition. His ribs jutted out of his pale skin. His breastbone caved into his chest and his belly protruded low between his hips. She removed his trousers to find his spinal column poking out in a straight line down to the concave remainder of his buttocks.

Iza felt sick. She had never seen a child in this condition still able to move about of his own will. Calluses had begun to form on the bony surfaces that protruded from his skin, caused by the incessant rubbing against shoes and clothing.

"Would you like a hot meal tonight," she asked.

He stood naked before her, his teeth chattering in the cold.

"No?"

"I'm not hungry, mama. Food gives me a tummy ache. It makes me go potty."

She smiled despite herself.

He would soon be unable to walk. Then what?

"We'll stay here awhile and rest. Then we must move on."

"Okay."

His eyes were haunted. Vacant. Izabel saw the familiar look of death in them.

That morning, they ate pan fish from the river and drank hot, black tea. Magda ate her share and what remained of her brother's. The children lay together in a ball to keep warm and, as soon as Magdalena's arms were around him, David fell fast asleep. Izabel whispered to her daughter.

"You must look after David. You must give him any food you can spare."

"I know, mama. I see."

Magda snuggled next to him and fell asleep. That night, Iza could not wake David. He lay on the cold ground, lethargic and unresponsive.

"Get up!" She shouted at him. "Get up you stupid boy. Do you want to die here? Get up!"

She smacked his face until he bleated. He struggled to lift himself off the ground.

"Good boy. Come on, David, it's not far now. Don't give up now. Your mother will be waiting for you. She will have your surprise. What was it?"

"A fire engine."

"Yes, a fire engine. I remember."

"And a red caboose."

"Of course."

He wobbled unsteadily on his feet.

"Magda, lift him onto my back. I will kneel and, David, you must climb up. I will give you a horsy ride!"

"We're not going to leave him, are we, Mama?"

"We won't leave him."

"Is he going to die?"

"Shut up! Put him on my back. Help me!"

For two nights, Izabel plodded south along the Tisza with one child strapped onto her front and another clinging around her neck. On the third day, David stopped eating altogether. Izabel pleaded, threatened and cajoled, but the child was too weak to even fight back.

She watched him breathing on the ground as she lifted her shirt to check on Jael. The baby smiled up at her mother. Her cheeks were flush with health, chubby legs kicking Iza's sunken stomach. She placed the baby on a patch of soft grass and went to where David lay in the dirt. She lifted him in her aching arms, lifted her shirt to expose a sagging breast, and placed it over his mouth. He feebly protested.

"I'm not a baby anymore."

"You are my baby now. My milk won't make you sick. Don't fight me, David. Please. I don't think I could bear it."

She squeezed a few drops of nourishment onto his lips.

"See? It's not so bad."

She forced him to drink, gagging on her milk, refusing to let him go free until the breast was dry, then holding him in her arms until he returned to his dreams. She whispered in his ear.

"Just a little further, child. Just a little further."

Jael began to cry just as Magdalena came into the clearing holding a handful of berries and two tiny brown eggs. Izabel's shoulders screamed as she began to build a shallow fire pit. She cooked the eggs in a spot of grease, mixing them with a slice of stale bread. Magdalena devoured her meal so hungrily that Izabel shared half of hers.

"You are a treasure to me, daughter. We wouldn't be here if not for you. I love you and Jael more than life itself. Do you know this?"

"Yes, mama."

"I made a promise to David's mother. Do you know what a promise is?"

"Yes, mama."

"I made a promise I would take care of her son. Your brother. I promised her I would save his life. I would risk everything to bring him home. Do you understand what I'm saying?"

"Yes, mama."

"I cannot go on, Magdalena. I cannot carry them both."

The light of understanding flashed in her child's eyes.

"I will carry Jael! Don't worry, mama, I will carry her for you. She is small and light, mama."

"She almost weighs as much as you now!"

"What will you do?"

"I will leave in awhile and take her to a farmhouse I saw off in the distance. It is not far from here. I saw the lights glowing warm in the farmhouse. It is a nice home, Magda. She is little. They will care for her and we'll return once we bring David to safety."

"No, mama."

"I must."

"No, mama. I won't let you."

"I have to or we'll die out here."

"I won't let you take her away from me!"

"Kiss your sister, Magda. I'm going now."

"*No, Mama!*"

She grabbed the infant's feet, nearly ripping her from her mother's arms.

"Please, Magda! You will see her again. I promise. You will see her again."

She snatched the baby from the girl's grasp and turned to leave, her young daughter running behind her.

"No, mama, no mama, no, mama!"

"Get away, or I'll beat you!"

She raised her hand to strike her daughter. Magdalena stopped dead in her tracks and stared at her mother with a look of sheer desperation. Her tiny hands clenched into tight fists and tears streamed down her face. Izabel turned away and continued toward the farmhouse.

"*I hate you!*"

She heard her daughter scream in the darkness, only once, and then there was silence.

I know, baby, I know.

She moved across the farmer's yard towards the barn. She knew the family would be up early if there were animals to tend. She slid open the barn door quietly and slipped inside. All was quiet except for the occasional whinny of a horse or the snuffling of a cow.

It was warm inside the great wooden walls. It was a good place. She settled into a corner of an empty stall, the smell of sweet timothy itching her nostrils, and began to undo the ties that bound her daughter to her breast. When she pulled the child away, she noticed that one breast was nearly dry. Izabel knew that unless she consumed more food, her milk would soon be gone. The other breast sagged limply over her sunken belly.

Though Jael had not yet endured the effects of slow starvation, she soon would, and she would not last as long without nutrition. The young and the old were always the first to suffer.

Her heart ached as she watched her daughter sleeping peacefully. She was perfection. She was Izabel's greatest accomplishment. How wicked to have been given so rare a gift, only to have it stolen away five months later.

It wasn't fair. Hot tears squeezed onto her cheeks. She held her nose to control her sobbing. The animals stared at her. She couldn't do it. She didn't know these people. She would never know if they loved her.

Or abused her.

She wouldn't see her walk, or talk, or be married. Izabel began to wrap a long rag around her left hand, crooning to her daughter as she did so.

Damn Eva! Damn her son! It is he who should suffer. Why should I abandon my child? Why, God? Why am I always made to pay for the sins of others? Why must I always struggle? Why have you abandoned me?"

She moved the rag over her child's sleeping face and pressed down firmly with both hands. The baby jerked spastically, flailing at her mother's hands with tiny fists, her cries nearly inaudible beneath the layers of cloth. Suddenly, her thrashing slowed, her breathing became shallow and her eyes flew open wide. She gazed up at her mother in surprise. Iza began to scream.

"I am a believer, a descendent of Abraham and Sarah, I am a true daughter of Israel. Why have you forsaken me?

Why have you abandoned us on our journey? Why must I choose between the life of my child and the son of a Jew? Why?"

Her voice was hoarse with screaming. She heard a dog barking in the direction of the house. She heard a man shouting.

"Hello? Come out of there. I won't hurt you."

Suddenly she gasped, jerking the cloth away from the baby's face. The child lay blue and lifeless on the ground. Iza shook her violently, but there was no response.

Dear God! What have I done?

She stumbled to her feet and crashed through the stall door, ripping a gash in her leg three inches across. Blinded by pain and grief, she ran headlong into the great wooden doors. A barn owl came swooping down from the rafters, flying on silent wings, to perch atop the crisscrossed beams above her daughter's shapeless form.

Iza was terrified. Rroma feared the owl for it was *bibaxt*, bad luck, to Gypsies; an evil portend of death. His great head rotated around to gaze at her. His enormous eyes looked coldly at her in the faded starlight that streamed in from the half-opened barn door. She hissed at him, waving her arms, attempting to draw him away from Jael.

She heard a man's voice draw closer. His lantern cast a thin light in the darkness.

"I see you, girl. What is this about? Are you hurt?"

She tensed at the sight of the gun, which he immediately lowered to the ground.

"There now, I won't hurt you. Come inside where it's warm. You can speak to my wife."

"Nikolai," she heard a woman's voice call.

"Bury her. Bury her with your dead."

Then she was gone.

When Izabel returned to their hiding place, she found Magdalena weeping alone on the ground. The girl jumped up into her mother's arms, smothering her with wet kisses.

"I thought you left me."

Izabel cupped the girl's chin in a trembling hand.

"Never. We must go, now. Quickly!"

She scooped David up in her arms and disappeared into the night, frantic voices calling in the darkness behind her.

"Little mother! Little mother!"

She moved fast; with renewed purpose. She knew she was cursed. The dead would soon come for her. They would find her and torment her soul. She must first bring the children to safety, fulfilling her promise to Eva. Fulfilling her destiny. Then she would make her amends to the dead.

Twenty

People living in a heightened state of fear have an amazing capacity to walk the narrow line between madness and despair. Human survival kicks in, robbing the brain of emotion, until the body is made safe. Only then does grief flood in to consume the soul.

Sarai was one of two hundred and eighteen of Mártély's Jews who survived the great fire. They survived the march to Szeged after the stragglers were shot and others were taken by exposure. Two hundred and eighteen was the final count documented by the Nazis after the relocation, after the cattle cars, after the final sorting at Auschwitz. But numbers can often be misleading.

A small unit of Germans was given orders to relocate Mártély's Jews 100 miles south to the train yards of Szeged. Several hours into the march, Sarai noticed a family of Rroma standing along the road with an Arrow Cross guard. There was a mother and father, four children and an old woman. They all stood along the road with their bags like they were waiting for the ten o'clock train to the picture show.

The Rroma watched as Mártély's Jews approached from the northwest. The children sucked on their thumbs and pinched each other, staring with dark, shining eyes. The Rromani father nodded to the men while his wife busied herself with their children. The grandmother stood behind the others, her eyes burning with anger. Once she passed the little family by, Sarai soon forgot them.

When the sun rose to its midday zenith, the group was allowed a rest. Sarai sank to her knees in relief; her daughter collapsing beside her. The women barely spoke. What was there to say? Sarai was still furious with her daughter for leaving David with the Rromani girl. And what of her son-in-law, Shimon?

There is another.

She glanced at Eva's swollen tummy.

I was too hard on her about the boy.

She offered Eva a bite of her bread, but her daughter barely moved. They sat on the grass for a long while. Sarai made conversation with the woman sitting beside her and Eva silently chewed a stick of gum.

"Did you know that in 1923, Germany owed more than thirty-one billion dollars in war debt? My husband Joseph said that German veterans of the Great War were deeply angered and humiliated when France and Belgium occupied the Ruhr, for Germany was economically broken, and could not make the annual installation of its war-reparations payments…" Sarai noticed one of the Rromani children wandering through the camp, begging for food. She was a small girl, no older than five.

"For shame," said Sarai. "Look at how filthy she is! It's a wonder she doesn't have scabies."

Scolding Sarai, the woman retorted, "Have pity, Sarai. I don't recall anything in our teachings that says poverty is a sin."

Eva turned her head slightly in the direction of the conversation, intrigued by the rare criticism of her mother.

"That's very noble of you to say, but your compassion is wasted on them, for as they take your food with one hand, they'll be picking your pocket with the other."

Someone handed the little girl a piece of fruit, which she immediately began to devour. She walked slowly through the crowd, tearing into an apple, juice running down her chin and dripping down the back of one hand. Her eyes moved inquisitively over the travel-weary families, pausing to linger over a little Jewish boy. She stared and chewed and stared some more.

What a rude little girl!

She wandered up to Sarai.

"Hello," she said, in Magyar tongue.

"Hello yourself. Aren't you going to share that food with your family? Maybe they're hungry too."

The little girl slowly removed the fruit from her smacking lips, shamefacedly wrapping it in her apron. She looked down at Sarai.

"Do you have any food to spare?"

"My goodness, child, you've been eating like a cow! Take a look around you. There are many hungry children here. What makes you so special?"

The woman sitting beside her cleared her throat. "Here's a piece of fruit."

"No. Let me give her some food, along with some tasty advice. The Lord will provide for those who serve others."

Sarai dug through her knapsack and retrieved a loaf of bread.

"Now, take this to your mother. And don't let me catch you sneaking a bite when you leave."

The girl took the bread hesitantly and then quickly rolled it up in her apron like a spider wraps a fly. She ran hastily through the crowd, barely remembering to say "thank you" as she went.

"No one can accuse me of mistreating the poor!"

The woman beside her rolled her eyes and continued to rub her feet.

Several hours later, Sarai caught sight of the little girl again, this time trailing a few steps behind her.

"Hi," she said shyly. Sarai ignored her, plodding ahead.

Eva smiled down at her. "Hi there," said Eva. "What's your name?"

"My name is Katarina. But my family calls me Kat."

"I see. What a beautiful name!"

Funny, I envisioned her more a pig. Sarai smiled to herself, pleased with the joke.

Sarai threw her a wry glance. "Are you hungry again, Kat?"

"I'm always hungry."

"Yes. I see that. What happened to the bread I gave you?"

"I gave that to my mama. They ate it all!" The girl beamed with pride.

"I have candy if you'd like a piece."

"Yes!"

"Make it last. I only have one bag."

Kat popped a piece of hard candy into her pink mouth and smiled. Eva laughed aloud at the sight of the gaping hole where the girl's front teeth should have been. Sarai turned away, head shaking, before anyone noticed the grin spreading across her face.

Kat moved up to visit them each day, and so Sarai began to enjoy their walks together. She was bright and inquisitive. Sarai wasn't sure if it was the company or the candy that kept the girl coming back. She didn't care.

The sassy child was a welcome distraction from what lay ahead in Szeged, and beyond. Sarai felt grateful for the illusion of normalcy, however minute. They might have been on a walking tour through a nature conservancy, except for the German troops keeping time with loaded rifles. Just when reality became a little too real, Katarina popped up between them.

Sarai wished she were at home baking cookies and sitting next to the stove, sharing a book and a cup of cider. She longed to leave her mark; if only she had a little more time. Engrossed in her prayers, Sarai startled to find the girl standing before her.

Kat looked at her, wide-eyed. "What are you doing?"

"I am praying. Don't you pray, Katarina?"

"No."

"Do your mother and father pray?"

"No."

"Would you like to pray with me?"

"Oh, yes!"

"Alright. Get down on your knees and clasp your hands together. Here, like this. Alright. Are you ready now?"

"I'm ready."

"The King Who rules over kings, in His compassion may He sustain them and protect them from every trouble, woe and injury. May he rescue them and put into their heart and into the heart of all their counselors compassion to do good with us and with all Israel, our brothers. In their days and our days, may Judah be saved and may Israel dwell securely, and may the Redeemer come to Zion. So may it be His will. And let us say, Amen."

When Sarai had finished her prayers, she glanced over at Kat. The child's eyes were clenched shut, her hands held fast, lips moving in kind. She slowly opened her eyes.

"I'm done."

"Very good. Did you like that?"

"I liked it very much."

"Katarina!" Her father called to her sharply. The child jumped to her feet to run to him.

"I hope she does not bother you?"

Eva said, "No sir, she is lovely." But the man continued looking at Sarai.

"N-no," she stammered, "she's not bothering me."

"If she bothers you, send her back to us."

"I will."

"Let's go." The girl skipped behind him while Sarai watched wistfully after her. "Good. Now for some peace and quiet."

Eva laughed. "Oh, mama. You know you like her."

"Like her? Hah! You know who she puts me in mind of, don't you? Maybe if I liked grubby little imps breathing all over me. Really."

"Oh, mama, did I do the right thing?" Eva burst out. "I don't even know if David's still alive."

"It's natural to wonder, Eva, but never doubt, for God expects our faith in all things. He will make a way for them."

"But how can she make it with three little ones?"

"Eva, I never took a liking to that girl as you had. You know that. However, I don't know a more resourceful person. She's been taught how to survive, moving about undetected, since she was small. The Gypsies are nomads, wanderers, it's in their blood. She'll be difficult to track, even by the soldiers."

"You're right, mama."

"If David was here with us, he would not have lived. The very old and the very young can't work. What use are they to the Germans? What use will I be?"

"What do you mean?"

"Witnesses say the dead walk in those camps. Once the trains are unloaded, the useless are separated out. One group lives. The other does not."

"Oh, mama."

"Your father and I are old. We've had a good life. We aren't afraid to die. But your children must be taught to respect our ways and honor those that went before them. God is in control. We can pray for His blessings, His protection, even His intervention. But I know that David lives, I know it in my heart. Let's just leave the worry to God."

So the days turned to night and the nights turned to days, and Mártély's Jews walked from first light until the earth was shrouded again in darkness. They walked until their feet blistered and their throats parched.

Tears squeezed out of the corners of Eva's eyes and her hands swelled until her fingernails were blue. But the Lord was good, for there was no blood. Sarai rubbed her daughter's aching body and held her when she cried for Shimon. For the first time in her life, Sarai felt utterly powerless.

Katarina hovered in the background with watchful eyes, quick to fetch water or bring fresh ticking for a pillow. The child's diminutive size made maneuvering easier because the guards paid little attention to her. Sarai thought the price of a piece of candy a small one to gain so loyal a helper.

The crowd waxed and waned as it poured over the roadway. The tension mounted with each passing day. Most shuffled ahead without a sound, but occasionally someone babbled, sobbed or laughed at nothing at all. The crowd closed in to absorb them in a loving embrace. Sometimes the outburst was ignored, sometimes not.

The remaining three hundred thirty-six Jews dragged into Szeged ten days later. They walked through the streets as the locals went about the mundane business of their lives. They passed men smoking cigarettes over a hotly contested game of checkers. They passed women clucking over the latest fashions in the store windows. They passed children shouting over a game of stickball.

When they arrived at the train yards, they collapsed, exhausted. The old guards left to find a hot meal and accommodations and a new set of angry faces moved in to replace them. The soldiers moved through the crowd, prodding people on to the receiving area. Eva maneuvered herself onto her hands and knees and tried to lift herself off the ground.

A young soldier screamed at her. "Get up, you fat cow!" He ran over to her and jerked her to her feet. Eva groaned and nearly fell, but was caught under one arm by Sarai.

"They are watching you, Eva. You must stand on your own. Ask God for strength; ask Him to carry you through. If you go down now, you'll never get up again."

The Nazis were efficient. A well-oiled machine. All three hundred thirty-six of Martely's Jews were processed, names, birthdates, and family backgrounds were catalogued, and suitcases, handbags, and trunks were searched and loaded onto a boxcar in under two hours.

Suddenly, chaos erupted. Families huddled together as soldiers drove them toward cattle cars. Mothers whirled about in a panic, calling to their wayward children. People poured through the darkened doorways like sand. Some of the men lifted their children into their mothers' waiting arms, others lingered behind to locate the missing.

Two men heaved Eva up off the platform, grunting with the effort. They called out to Sarai, who seemed distracted by the madness. She saw Katarina racing around the platform, screaming for her mother, as the soldiers began to crack people over the head. Her eyes rolled wildly, searching faces, as people shoved her to and fro.

"Katarina," Sarai called.

"*Katarina!*"

Kat turned in the direction of the voice, smiling in anticipation of her mother's face. Her face fell in disappointment at seeing the old woman.

"I can't find my mother."

"Come here, child," she said. Two soldiers began walking across the platform towards them.

"Is she yours?"

Sarai hesitated.

"No."

One of them screamed at her. "Get on the train!"

The child was unceremoniously tossed into a railcar. The two men who helped Eva quickly pulled the old woman aboard before the doors slammed behind her. Sarai heard the child crying through the open clapboards as the padlocks were being fastened to the outside. The train shuddered once before it lurched on to its final destination. Aushwitz.

For three days, the cars rumbled across the picturesque countryside with human beings packed ten-deep inside. The bodies of the sick, dead and dying, pressed together like kernels of corn, stood freezing in their own juices. The stench of urine, feces and vomit wafted through the cars. Finally, the great engine wound down and came to a halt at the camp. The doors were slid open and the cars were unloaded of their contents.

Mártély's Jews staggered out, blinking in the sunlight like emerging coal miners. They stood shivering on the snow-covered ground within sight of the great iron gates. Many clung together as a German officer began moving through the crowd to inspect the living.

Thud.

Thud.
Thud.
The dead were rolled off the cars onto the ground below—many were children who had frozen solid. Sarai searched for the clothing of one child, and was grateful not to find her.

The officer began inspecting prisoners, checking their eyes and teeth and mouths, and then forming two distinct groups. He brushed past the two women with hardly a glance, directing them to the group on the right. Sarai squeezed her daughter's arm so hard her fingertips left dents in the gooseflesh. She was relieved to see so many able-bodied Jews in their midst.

So, not yet?

Sarai looked up just in time to see the bodies of a woman and her infant being thrown from a boxcar. Katarina appeared from nowhere to rush to her mother's side, wailing like an air-raid siren. A German soldier scooped her up and carried her to the opposite side, where she stood alone, weeping, her father nowhere in sight.

A German soldier took the final count.

"Two hundred and eighteen, sir!"

"Two hundred and eighteen? Good."

Sarai watched the oldest, youngest and weakest begin the walk towards certain death. She leaned over and kissed her daughter on the cheek.

"I love you, Eva. Tell your father I said goodbye."

"Where are you going?"

Sarai hurried after the departing group.

"*No!*"

Sarai broke through the crowd that surrounded her and marched straight past the German officer to clasp Katarina's tiny hand in her own.

"No, mama," cried Eva.

"Shut up," a man hissed.

Sarai never looked back. They walked towards the roaring furnaces beyond the razor-wire fence. When they reached the showers, she knelt in front of the child who trembled naked before her.

"Do you remember how we did it last time?"

The girl nodded and closed her eyes as Sarai began to pray.

"The King Who rules over kings, in His compassion may He sustain them and protect them from every trouble, woe and injury. May He rescue them and put into their heart and into the heart of all their counselors compassion to do good with us and with all Israel, our brothers. In their days and our days, may Judah be saved and may Israel dwell securely, and may the Redeemer come to Zion. So may it be His will. And let us say, Amen."

The child moved her lips, her hands clasped together. The gas began to pour into the room. The others screamed, running for the doors, beating and clawing and crying out, then falling like a house of cards, as the gas overcame them.

"Don't be afraid, Katarina. I am with you."

Some time later, workers began pulling bodies out of the chamber with ice picks. Though one worker fought to separate the bodies of an old woman and child, he could not, so he shoved them into the ovens together, staring at their faces as the flames consumed them.

Twenty-one

A capable-looking, middle-aged woman approached from the center aisle, glancing sideways at the numbered rows as she walked. She breezed up to Magdalena in seat 18C and asked to scoot in by the window. Magda jumped to her feet.

"Yes. Of course."

The woman raised a slender arm over her head to slide a carrying case into the overhead bin, and then picked up her purse from Magda's seat. In one fluid motion, she sat down, shut the window shade, and pivoted the blower onto her face. She smiled politely when she noticed Magda watching her.

"I have an extra magazine if you'd like."

"Thank you."

Magda fidgeted with her seatbelt, lifting the latch up and dropping it down again.

Click. Click. Click.

"Never flown before?"

"How could you tell?"

"Oh, no reason. You just seemed a little nervous, that's all."

A stewardess moved purposely through the cabin, reminding passengers to fasten their safety belts. Magda watched as she handed out pillows and blankets and helped load bags into the overhead compartment.

"I'll have a Chardonnay, please."

"Umm, ma'am, we haven't taken off yet."

"Yes, I see that."

"We'll begin serving beverages as soon as we're safely in the air."

"C'mon. Give me a break, will you? All I need is one tiny bottle. I'll be discreet, I promise."

"I'm sorry, ma'am. Our policy states…"

"Alright! You can go now."

She dismissed her with a wave of her hand.

The woman gave Isabel a sly smile. "I have something to take the edge off, but if you got caught with it in the restroom, you might be forced to share."

"No, thank you, I don't smoke."

"I was kidding. You really are tense, aren't you?"

Magda's face burned with embarrassment.

"What do you do?"

"I'm an editorial assistant at a news service here in the southwest suburbs. What about you?"

"I'm a musician. I play violin in the New York City Philharmonic. I'm headed home from visiting a college roommate; she lives in Evanston now."

"Really? How impressive."

"Not really. I'm just second-chair. Someone would have to die for me to move up. The pay is shit, but I love my work. The people are great; truly awe-inspiring. You understand the culture, don't you? I mean, being that you're sort of a writer."

"The only culture I get is the bacteriological kind from the sushi bar my editor frequents."

"You said you were an assistant editor?"

"I'm an *editorial assistant*. The difference is about $30,000.00 a year in salary and benefits. I regurgitate press releases for a weekly food column. I compile a weekly 'Around Town' column where I get to play God—well, maybe just a Demigod. I hold power of pen over the meetings of the Sons of Norway Polar Star Lodge and performances by the Silk and Thistle Scottish Country dancers. This would be considered a stellar week."

The woman laughed aloud. "You're hilarious! How about that magazine?"

The women chatted awhile over current events before the musician retired to her book. Magda lay back in her seat sipping a drink, thinking about the recent events in her life.

The neighborhood cronies she'd met at the Rheinlander for lunch that day told Madga how her mother happened upon Pieter on a New York City street while he was there on business; apparently quite by accident.

Immigration officials required proof that David's family was unlocatable, so for weeks they lived in a fleabag motel on 103rd Street while she scrubbed toilets at a four-star in Queens. It was a humiliating time for Izabel. She was alone in a strange land, uneducated and unskilled. Every day she left her children alone so she could scratch out a living while the government beaurocrats pushed their papers.

Pieter took one look at Iza's condition and insisted she accompany him to dinner. When she mentioned Shimon's son was still alive, he demanded to see him with his own eyes. He lifted the little boy in his arms and cried like a baby, smothering kisses on the child's yellow mop.

"It's a miracle, Izabel."

"Is it?"

She asked the question to no one in particular as her daughter stared from a corner of the kitchen.

The next day, Pieter cancelled his return flight to pay a visit to the immigration office and, within a week, three new resident aliens came home to Pigeon Hill, eager for a new beginning.

Pieter opened a bedroom in his own home to the little family, and also gave Izabel a job at his bakery on East Downer Place. He remained protective, questioning her when she was out, hovering close when she was with him. He bought her fine clothes and shoes, feathered hats and gold earrings, wanting only a smile in return for his generosity.

The neighbors who'd once embraced her now embarked on a whispering campaign concerning the nature of their relationship. One early evening, when Izabel was shopping for produce at Jungel's Grocery in Aurora's mid-town, she overheard several of her neighbors gossiping in the dry goods aisle.

"Bethany saw Izabel lying naked on her bed at Pieter's house last week?"

"Yes, yes! I heard that too."

"Will Izabel stop at nothing to have a man keep her? That woman is a menace to our community. She's nothing less than a whore!"

"My God. The children!"

"I'm more concerned about Pieter. Izabel will certainly disappear with his money. She is a Gypsy, you know."

Iza began to sequester herself inside of the house.

Several weeks later, his bachelor friend, Josef, spoke to Pieter in private. "Forgive me for prying, Pieter."

"What's on your mind?"

"I don't know how to say this…delicately."

"What is it that you wish to ask me, Josef?"

"What exactly are your intentions with that Gypsy woman?"

"What in God's name do you mean?"

"Well, the people in our community have noticed you spending a great deal of money on Izabel and her children."

"Does this seem out of the ordinary to you? I have helped many of those…less fortunate souls…recently arrived from Hungary and Romania."

"How do I say this, Pieter?"

"What is it you wish to ask me?"

"I do not wish to offend."

"Out with it."

"Do you desire something more from Izabel in return for your obvious affection? I ask you this as your dear friend, Pieter."

"H-how dare you! How dare you question my integrity?"

"It is not just me, Pieter. Many of the families on Pigeon Hill are…well…concerned about your welfare. Concerned with how you'll be perceived."

"Devils!" Pieter flew into a terrific rage, tearing about the bakery, turning over cake pans and stainless steel bowls, proclaiming his bitter defense. Izabel silently ran out the back door and was not seen for days.

The county health department visited the home about childhood vaccinations, social workers rang to discuss school enrollment, but Izabel would speak to no one. No one knew what went on inside that house.

Pieter's attitude began to change. He barked at Izabel when she struggled to lift baking pans, demanding that she move faster. He accused her of neglect when she dawdled getting home. He began to force her own children to stay away from her, chasing them out of the bakery and down the street when they came to visit her.

Magdalena kept watch over her half-brother. She seemed to know that her mother was in a bad place. Suspicious neighbors suddenly tried to befriend her, but she shied away from them; they'd already alienated Magdalena beyond her trusting. Even the parish priest from St. Nicholas began calling.

At this point within the lengthy oral history, the old women of Pigeon Hill clasped their hands together in jubilation, and their eyes misted over with tears of joy, for a letter had arrived from Sheffield, England. Eva had survived Auschwitz. She was coming to America to collect her son. And, at that very moment, it became painfully obvious to Magdalena how loved Eva had been. Loved by the very same community that had so reviled her own mother. Eva was a miracle...a living testament to God. To the old women, it was as if Eva had been resurrected from the dead all over again.

Pieter seemed relieved to receive the news, not only in his eagerness to see Eva, but because Izabel's behavior bordered on the bizarre. Her hair was disheveled and her clothes unwashed. Her eyes skittered about, jittery and out-of-focus, awash in the red hue of fatigue.

Pieter looked at her with disgust and screamed, "You smell like a sow, Izabel, go home and wash yourself. Don't return until you do. This is a place of business, for God's sake."

Josef's fears were confirmed when he happened upon a strange scene one night after the bakery had closed. Josef rapped lightly on the front door. Not hearing a response, he tip-toed through the dark storefront. He maneuvered past a small dining table when he heard Pieter taunting Izabel in the kitchen while she prepared the morning bread to rise. She worked in silence, seemingly deaf to his words.

"I know about you. I know how you laid with Shimon and bore him two children. What happened to the other one, Iza? What did you do? The rumors are flying, girl, and if there is any truth to them, there will be a reckoning. I've tried to help you. I took pity on you. I took your children in as if they were my own, yet you show me no affection. Am I disgusting to you? I give you an opportunity and you spit in my face."

She whirled about and screamed at him. Josef was so stunned he fell against a chair, but the noise was masked by the shrieking of her voice.

"I hate you. I hate all of you. Stay away from me. You are no friend to me. You are like all the others, Pieter. *You* are the pig. Don't touch me again, or I swear I will kill you. There is no hope for me. God's mercy has passed from my sight. Do you really think your idle threats scare me?"

Her laughter made Josef's hair stand on end.

"Don't touch me again. I owe you nothing."

She darted out the door. Pieter stood before his friend; shocked to silence.

"She's crazy," Pieter finally managed to say. He laughed nervously. "My wife and children have all gone. I am alone in this world. My only joy comes in helping others like me. I should never have taken her into my home. Ungrateful bitch." He continued to spew. "I've done nothing wrong. Everyone here knows me. I have helped every family on Pigeon Hill. You know me! For God's sake, Josef, say something!"

The Aurora police escorted Pieter out of his home later that evening for a chat, and the young priest followed soon after to speak to the girl. Izabel locked herself inside her room and drew the shades. Both children huddled with her under the bedcovers.

Iza hissed at the priest like an animal when he entered her room. Suddenly, she flew across the floor, bare-skinned and bony, gibbering unintelligibly about ghosts. Both children cowered in a corner as the priest struggled to cover her with a sheet, screaming over his shoulder to call an ambulance.

Izabel was still committed at Mercy Hospital when Eva came to take her son. Eva lay next to Izabel, bound and sedated in bed. She petted her shorn head while Iza wailed in her arms.

"It's all over now. Everything will be alright. You'll see."

Magdalena remembered none of it, but at least now she understood. She understood why Pieter climbed on top of her mother late at night; how his pervasive loneliness and sense of entitlement found opportunity in the powerlessness of Izabel's past. She understood her mother's anguish over the choice she made over her own child; how it haunted and compelled her to madness.

But whatever became of the women's love for each other? Why did they not live out their lives together; raising children, remarrying, and growing old together? What forces held sway over Iza, compelling her to return to the ashes of her past?

Why was I left behind? Why was I abandoned by the woman who had risked everything to save me?

She knew she would soon have her answers.

Twenty-two

David watched the vehicle lights flashing around his window shade. For more than three hours he lay in bed, unable to sleep, passing the time counting cars as they drove past. He was up to forty-five vehicles now.

Doesn't anyone sleep anymore?

He flopped on his side and squinted at the alarm clock. 3:33 a.m. He stared at the illuminated dial. 3:34 a.m. 3:35 a.m. 3:36 a.m. He kicked off the covers in disgust, swinging his feet onto the hardwood floor.

Dumb-dumb stood up from his nest in a pile of unfolded laundry in the corner. He arched his back and yawned lazily. He pulled his claws in and out along the wooden floor, meowing plaintively at David's shapeless form on the bed. David shuffled to the bathroom, blinking in the harsh, overhead lights. He scratched himself as he urinated, shook himself off, and then stumbled downstairs to the kitchen.

David set the automatic coffeemaker to brew and sat at the kitchen table, picking up the plane tickets he had laid there the night before. He had a ticket for Magdalena and one for himself, to Budapest, Hungary on United flight

187—first-class, of course. His nerves were beginning to fray. He guessed Magda was also lying wide-awake in her bed, and he considered calling her before she left for O'Hare.

He went to his study instead and booted up his desktop. A former lover, on staff at the New York City archive, had saved dozens of data files about the Rroma in Eastern Europe onto a floppy disk at his request.

"New case," he told her.

He sat in front of the flickering screen, trying to determine the cultural climate that played a part in Izabel's admission to the asylum after the death of her infant. Frankly, he thought it a miracle she survived at all.

David surmised that one probable cause for Iza's instability might lie in her core value system. The belief in the supernatural was fundamental, a dreadful knowing that permeated the very fabric of Rromani society, from cradle to grave.

His correspondent had confirmed that female spirits, or fates, called the *vursitorja* by Rroma, were said to hover in a child's presence for three days after its birth to determine its future destiny and influence the choice of name by the parents. A red thread, called the *loli dori*, was then tied around the newborn's ankle or wrist and worn for two or three years afterwards to guard against the *jakhalo* or "evil eye."

Sighing, David considered how, for the Rroma, a pure state could only be achieved by maintaining spiritual balance in one's life and by avoiding shame. Not doing so may result in being declared unclean or, in extreme cases, being shunned by the community. Avoiding shame involved, among other things, demonstrating *patjiv*, or respect, to the elders.

David learned that maintaining spiritual harmony pleased the ancestral spirits, or *mulé*. The ancestral spirits were there to safeguard Rroma and help them remain pure. However, if the *mulé* were displeased, they would administer a punishment, or a warning signal called *prikaza*, by way of retribution. Depending on the nature of the offense, the reprisal may be mild, or so severe as to involve sickness, or even death.

Inhaling deeply, David wondered how the consequences of *prikaza* underlie the universal Rromani belief that nothing happened simply by chance. *Prikaza* brought bad luck and illness and could even be attracted by mingling with those thought to be unclean. This was the fundamental reason why Rroma avoided intimate contact with non-Rroma.

David read that, in a few isolated Rromani populations, death was seen as an unnatural occurrence that should anger those who pass away. Great extremes were taken to make amends before the time of death. There could be no risk of a hidden envy or secret resentment before the person began the journey to the world of the dead. The dying were never left alone. They were never allowed to pass away inside their own homes. Mirrors were covered and vessels containing water were emptied.

Feeling some disgust, he also read that, once dead, the body could not be touched, for fear of contamination. The nostrils of the deceased were plugged with beeswax or pearls to prevent evil spirits from entering the body.

Clothes, tools, jewelry and money were placed inside the coffin to be used in the journey from life.

After burial, all material ties were often destroyed. Clothes and linens were burned. Plates, cups, glasses and jewelry were broken or mutilated. Sometimes, animals belonging to the deceased were killed. No trace of the deceased could remain anywhere. Even the person's name was avoided unless absolutely necessary within these isolated Rromani communities.

Had Izabel feared the dead would return to seek revenge on the living? Was she afraid of retribution? Fair reasoning for madness? Perhaps. Reclusive behavior? No doubt.

Dumb-dumb thumped down the stairs to curl around David's leg as he worked in the pre-dawn stillness. As David continued to research the anatomy of the Rroma, he saw chilling parallels between their history and his own.

David nodded his head in recognition, for the Rroma, like the Jews, excluded outsiders, fanning suspicion by locals. Like the Jews, the Gypsies were accused of stealing babies for nefarious purposes. Like the Jews, Rroma were blamed for the spread of the bubonic plague, and came under attack from people like Martin Luther and Charles Darwin. Like the Jews by the Egyptians, Rroma were enslaved in Romania until the 1860's. Discrimination is frighteningly indiscriminate with the dark-skinned and the foreign.

Stranger yet, David's research uncovered weird Biblical references within several ancient Rromani beliefs. Some claimed to be descended from Noah. Others claimed to be the true descendents of Abraham and Sarah.

But the most widespread legend concerning the nomadic Rroma was based on the story of the crucifixion. According to legend, many people were asked to forge the nails of the cross, but all refused when they heard the purpose for which the nails were to be used. Finally, some Rromani blacksmiths agreed to make them. Because of this, Rroma were condemned to wander the earth forever.

According to David's research, however, linguistic and historical evidence supported the theory that Rroma originated in Northern India. Originally assembled to fight the Islamic armies of Mahmud of Ghazni, they were drawn from many different ethnic groups speaking a wide variety of languages.

Though comprised of lower castes and African mercenaries, they were made honorary members of the Kshattriya, "Warrior Caste." They exited India through the mountain passes and west into Persia between 1001 and 1027, battling Muslim forces all along the eastern limits of Islam.

Since their exodus, Rroma were outlawed, enslaved, hunted, tortured and murdered.

David sympathized that the Gypsies were called traitors to Christian countries, spies in the pay of the Turks, carriers of the plague, practitioners of witchcraft, and kidnappers of children. They were vagabonds and evildoers, Bohemians and cannibals. They were the "ballast of Humanity," "work shy," and social misfits. The Church was no asylum: Rromani children were not christened and the dead were not buried.

The Gypsies were forced to settle, work, reform and assimilate. In 1773, the Empress of Hungary ordered all

Rromani children over the age of five to be taken from their parents. They were sent to distant villages to be raised by peasants for 12 florins a year. Most ran away to rejoin their families, who took refuge in the mountains, or disappeared into the plains.

It sickened him that the presence of Gypsies was signaled from village to village by the ringing of church bells. The local population employed mutilation and branding to identify the nomadic Rroma. The cutting off of ears was especially favored. Information agencies were later established to report on Rromani movement: national registries, photographs, fingerprints, genealogical information and police surveillance were all carefully documented in the public's best interest.

This is strong stuff to swallow all at once. David forced himself to take a break. He savored the taste of the Scotch whiskey as it traveled along his tongue to the back of his throat. Once he began to feel liquid burn of alcohol through his veins, and the muscles along his jaw began to loosen nicely, David returned to his computer to finish reading the intensive research.

The subject matter didn't improve much for his absence, however, for in January of 1934, the Rroma in Germany began to be sterilized by injection and castration. Two years later, race hygienist Dr. Robert Korber wrote, "The Jews and the Gypsies are today remote from us because of their Asiatic ancestry, just as ours is Nordic." On August 2, 1944, four thousand Rroma were gassed and cremated in a single action at Auschwitz-Birkenau during "Gypsy Night." Referred to by Rroma as *O Porrajmos*, 'the Great Devouring,' more than one and a half million Gypsies were killed in Europe by the Nazi regime and puppet states.

David felt emotionally exhausted. Like the rain and the wind, the earth and the moon, the Jews and the Gypsies were inexorably linked, bound through time, circumstance and perception. The friendship between his mother and Iza seemed less unlikely now. No matter how you cut it, meat was meat in the slaughterhouse. Fiber, tendon, bone, sinew and blood had no bearing on the butcher.

They were just two insignificant women in a race against public opinion.

David sat alone with his bottle of Scotch and began to ruminate on the essence of humanity. "We are varying degrees of a universal, a principle bound by purpose, a distillation of a creator's mad fancy. Mankind's greatest achievement lies in service to the vulnerable, the poor, and the weak. Mankind's greatest downfall lies in its unwillingness to do so. In this, we will be ultimately judged by God. Elitism has no stroke in death. Arrogant pursuits always lead to spiritual ruin. Life is the great leveler. An insignificant girl's desire to protect the life of a condemned boy so eloquently illustrated that fact."

David owed his very existence to a lowly Gypsy. *A woman!* He intended to repay his debt.

Twenty-three

One week after Eva's mother was burned inside the crematorium at Auschwitz she aborted the baby.

"It won't be easy, or clean, and the pain will be great. But this child won't survive a day beyond the womb. A guard will drown it in a bucket outside of the room where you lay bleeding."

The women whispered loudly in the dark sleeping quarters of Women's Block 28 as Eva wept with huge, convulsive sobs. The women tried to comfort her, petting her shorn head, and rubbing her aching back.

"You've suffered, little sister, we know. But you have to trust us. We can help you to survive, but there is no hope for this child. There is no food and the water is tainted. Typhus spreads through camp like the plague."

"You have to be able to stand in place for hours or you will be beaten. If they see weakness, they will shoot you. You are young. You can have more children. But this can only happen if you live. What good are a dead wife and mother to anyone?"

"I will not have more children. My husband and son are missing. I fear they are dead. This child is all I have left. I cannot kill him."

"Alright, don't get upset, Eva. But consider the life you give him. Pain, hunger, cold and then death. You are not to blame here. You will carry no guilt."

"I won't do it. Please don't make me."

"Quiet now. We'll talk again later."

The next day, Eva nearly dropped during morning roll call. She swayed on her aching feet and her fingertips tingled, but she gritted her teeth and held on. That night, the women chided her again to rid herself of her infant. They said it drained her of spare nutrients. She screamed at them to shut up and leave her alone. The women shrugged their shoulders, and shook their heads incredulously.

"She won't last a month," one woman whispered.

Her friend responded, "She is the mother and it is her choice. I've seen her. She is a strong one. She will choose to live."

"We cannot wait much longer. The child grows bigger with each passing day."

"It's her decision. Leave her be."

Three days later, Eva went down, crumbling in a heap upon the frozen ground.

Furious, a guard screamed at her. "Get her out of here!"

Eva groaned as she was lifted back on her feet by two prisoners. "Drop again, little mother, and you will not get back up."

"I told you to take care of this," the guard said to Eva's bunkmate.

"Yes, ma'am," the woman mumbled.

She hissed at Eva as she pulled her away from the formation. "You see? Now you get me in trouble!"

Two female prisoners dragged Eva back to the barracks and lay her down in her bunk. Eva moaned. "My belly feels heavy."

The older of the two women pressed down on her hard stomach.

"You are having contractions. You will lose it anyway. Your body cannot carry the child any longer. Let us take care of her for you."

Eva whispered through her pain. "Please take care of her."

"What's that?"

"Give her a proper burial."

"I will."

Two vials of morphine appeared from the inner lining of the older woman's uniform. "I snuck this from the infirmary at great risk to myself, Eva. It will help." The woman injected the contents into one thigh.

"Don't worry, I was a nurse. I won't hurt you."

"Just do it quickly."

Those were the last words she spoke before drifting off into a dream state. She floated along the ceiling, gazing down, fascinated, at the women working over her. She saw her thighs jerking in spasms as the nurse hastily dug inside her. She called to the other woman sharply as blood poured over her hand onto the concrete floor.

Was that a child's cry?

She saw herself shivering in the hay strewn about the wooden bunk.

"Wait."

She cried out, but the words did not come. She heard herself start to moan.

"Wait!"

She screamed silently in her mind.

"No, no, no!"

The room was silent.

"It is finished."

"She's still bleeding."

"She'll bleed for many days. But she'll live."

"I'll get some rags to stop the blood.

Silence.

"What do I do with it?"

"Wrap it in rags and give it to the guard. She will dispose of it."

"We promised to bury her."

"And how do you propose we do that?"

She felt a tugging sensation between her legs, and heard the younger woman choking back tears.

"Hurry! She'll be awake soon."

Eva lay on the bunk, awake and alone.

For many days afterward, Eva felt the tiny ghost inside of her. She still felt the swollen breasts, the aching back and the puffy ankles.

When she finally went away, she took Eva's taste, her sleep, her laughter, her joy, her sanity, her peace, her God. She left Eva with an ocean of tears and with the dreams of a child unrealized. She left her with loving regret.

Twenty-four

My Dearest Eva,
I have been feeling very sad these last weeks at the Shuleva summer home. Sofia gave me a writing journal yesterday. She said that if I wrote down my thoughts and feelings, it would help me to keep my spirits up. I just hope it keeps the spirits of the dead out of my dreams and keeps your spirit alive in my heart. My thoughts are of you and the others I left behind. I do not know where you are or even if you are still alive.

How ironic that so long ago you taught a young Rromani girl to read and write, and now she is the only living witness to your son's freedom and rise to manhood. My mother used to say 'one simple act of kindness reaps rewards far beyond our own understanding.'

David's health is fast-improving. He was very sick when we arrived in Djála. I did what I had to do to ensure he return to you—in God's time. He's a good boy. A smart boy. I know he will be of great comfort to you as my daughter has been to me.

I have done a terrible thing, Eva. There was an accident. I panicked. And now she is gone—my Jael—she is lost forever. She calls to me in my dreams. I can hear her in the moments just before I drift off to sleep. Sometimes I snap awake at night, I jerk up in my bed and I cry out to her, but she just recedes back into darkness.

I frightened the children so badly that they moved me to a separate room. Sofia comes in with cold compresses and Nikolay puts on some tea. They have been very kind to me, Eva, but I still miss my mother.

I received word that every Rrom in camp had been slaughtered by soldiers. Every man, woman and child. Do you remember that dreadful night? Why am I still alive? Why did God let me live? There were many other people, good people, who perished, yet the wicked continue to live.

Maybe it wasn't God's choice, maybe it was simply an accident, a mistake, a cosmic blunder, like the ant that slips through the sidewalk crack and escapes the shoe bearing down on it. I wish someone would explain it to me. Explain how this is possible. My heart feels heavy with it. I don't know how much longer I can carry this burden.

The Shuleva family hid us in their farmhouse for many weeks. Once they were certain we weren't followed, we traveled by car along the Danube River across Romania to their ancestral home on the shores of the Black Sea, in the seaport of Varna, in Bulgaria. The countryside was in ruins. But the war is nearing an end. God is good, indeed.

It has been a long, terrible journey for many. The countryside reeks of death and decay. The infrastructure has collapsed. Roads, buildings and bridges are all gone. Driving through the landscape, I was struck by a sense of the apocalyptic in this time and place. Though it may not be the end for mankind, it is certainly the end of its innocence. If it weren't for the kindness of Sofia and Nikolay, I would feel all decency was lost forever in this terrible war.

I sit here alone in the cottage by the sea. Though I think sad thoughts of those who've gone away, I strangely feel as though you are not far from me. I feel you close to my heart, though my mind is clouded by doubt. Do not worry about your son, Eva; I will love him as my own. Everything I have belongs to David. His mother had mercy on us. She gave us hope.

Nikolay seeks asylum for us in America. So, I sit and wait, hopeful for a future for our children. My journey is not yet over. Like the swallow that returns each year to Capistrano, I, too, will find my way home again.

I sit in silence, wondering at the miracle of life. Do you remember the Greek myth of Polymela that you once read to me in our secret garden in Mártély? Sophocles wrote of the young woman Polymela, who was brutally raped by her brother-in-law, a Thracian king. After he raped her, he cut out her tongue to keep her from telling his wife, her sister, what had happened. The desperate Polymela used the only means she had available, her wooden shuttle, to speak for her, weaving the scenes of her rape and mutilation into a tapestry. When her sister saw it, she understood, and she exacted a terrible revenge on the king.

We are each a single thread in His loom. The Weaver's hands fly and His right foot taps on the treadle. Back and forth, the wooden shuttle flies from right hand to left and back again, between the even threads of warp. Swiftly, the threads of warp crisscross each other, catching fast the thread the shuttle leaves behind.

And the tapestry stretches out for generations. The pattern appears random when seen up close, but divine understanding brings about order and beauty in its perfection.

I will write in my journal each day. I will keep alive the news of David and Magdalena and our adventures in America. We will be waiting for you, sister. I will find the courage to meet each day anew. I will work hard. I will not forget you.

Your Izabel

Twenty-five

The Germans ran about, hurrying to clean up their mess, once they heard the rattling of keys at the door. More than four thousand Jews were shot in advance of the Red Army, and massive, on-foot evacuation of prisoners and slave laborers began in earnest. On January 27, 1945, Soviet troops liberated the Auschwitz-Birkenau death camp. Only seven thousand inmates remained, including David's mother, Eva.

Word of the impending liberation raced through the camp like wildfire. The women wanted to shout praises to the Lord, but they had to keep their joy well-hidden, for any outburst, any laughter, any clapping or dancing, was soon met with a bullet in back of the head.

The desperate Nazis no longer bothered using cover of darkness to hide the naked bodies shuffling through the woods to the ovens. They didn't try to mask the screams of mothers and children with cheerful, familiar melodies played by the camp orchestra. Day and night, the chimneys belched out black smoke, and ashes rained down on their heads like some hellish snow.

When the Russian Army was within range, artillery shells screamed overhead and mortars thumped the frozen ground, and the sky glowed red with illumination rounds, allowing prisoners brief glimpses of the guards scurrying to escape.

Like rats on a sinking ship.

A female guard ran screaming into Eva's barracks, spraying Mosin-Nagant rounds about the room. The women pressed their trembling bodies tightly against the barracks walls, using the wooden bunks to shield the bullets, praying for God's mercy. Praying to live one more minute. One more hour. One more day.

When the Russians entered the camp, they found hundreds of survivors wandering in a daze. They shivered in their prison stripes, their heads shaved and eyes sunken with exhaustion. The women didn't cheer, or celebrate, or raise their hands in victory. Was it really over? Were they still alive?

As Eva watched, one middle-aged Polish woman fell to the ground, and wailed and beat her chest. A boy grabbed greedily at bread offered by the exhausted soldiers. Eva ate a piece of the bread and immediately collapsed.

A Russian soldier carried her limp body to a transport vehicle, his face twisted by fury, and grief. Suddenly, a well of emotion boiled up from the depths of her soul. She cried bitterly. She gnashed her teeth. She beat her tiny fists against his soiled uniform.

He lifted Eva into the back of the truck where she fell into a corner. She was handed a wool blanket and a handful of sugar cubes. An officer yelled at the men on the ground to stop handing out bread, for their skeletal bodies would die of shock from eating solid food.

Eva noticed a young girl, beautiful and sad, smiling at her a few feet away. She held out her hand and the girl crawled to her, curling up beside her beneath the army blanket. Eva cried in the girl's arms, but the girl was silent, sitting patiently.

"My mother is dead," she said matter-of-factly. "She had the typhus, so they shot her."

"Dear God!" Eva smoothed the girl's knotted hair as best she could.

"She is dead and I'm alone now. I'm alone now. I'm alone now."

Then Eva saw her bloody fingernails. The girl had pulled her hair out a strand at a time. She already had bare patches of scalp peeking out from her dull brown waves. A Russian officer noticed the bloody strands of hair clinging to her shirt and he growled at her.

"You there, stop that."

The girl smiled at him sweetly while continuing to dig near her ear. He muttered under his breath, and flopped onto a pile of boxes. The truck lurched down the road, over potholes and debris, towards the Slovakian border. The girl sucked her sugar cubes and pulled out her hair as Eva rocked her, crying inconsolably.

When they arrived at a makeshift hospital, Red Cross workers moved quickly to dispatch the sick and dying to hospital beds. Wishing to rid themselves of the body lice crawling over their skin, hundreds of people lined up outside to be disinfected. When the nurses saw the gaping hole in the scalp above the girl's left ear, they immediately whisked the child away, never to be seen again.

The attendants escorted Eva to a great room filled with other survivors. She curled up on a cot with her shoes still on. Not even her hunger, or the lice, or the crying of children could wake her. She slept for two days, waking in the early evening.

When she sat up in bed and coughed into her hands, Eva's gums oozed blood, her teeth rotten from malnutrition. Immediately, a nurse stood over her.

"How do you feel?"

Eva shook her head.

"Do you speak English?"

She managed a feeble, "Yes."

"I work for the Red Cross. My name is Helen, and I'm here to help. Do you have a place to stay? Do you have money?"

"I have no money. I have no home."

"We can help you with that." She paused. "Do you need help finding anyone? Is your family missing?"

"I must find my sister. She is caring for my son. I think they've gone to America."

"It will take some time, but I think we can locate them. First, let's start with your name."

Helen clicked her pen and began scribbling in a file. On a wheeled cart next to Eva's bed were hundreds of identical files.

It took the Red Cross three weeks to find Izabel in America. It would have taken longer without the information provided by the family in Bulgaria ... and without the paper forgeries obtained by Shimon in Pest so long ago. Izabel's temporary visa had been granted under an assumed identity. The resulting uproar when a second Eva Szótemel applied for a visa was a blessing, for suddenly the U.S. State Department was keen on locating the Gypsy who'd obtained false papers, and entered U.S. soil, illegally.

The immigration office in Chicago wasted no time contacting Iza's sponsor who, Eva was shocked to learn, was her old friend, Pieter. He picked her up from Chicago's central station, squeezing her bony fingers as they walked along the train platform.

"I have a surprise, Eva."

She clutched her bag tightly to her chest.

"It's a miracle."

"He's alive," she whispered.

"He's waiting for us."

Eva felt her knees buckle under her. Pieter caught her elbow, and she burst into tears.

"He's alive! Praise God!"

The thirty-seven miles to Aurora stretched out forever. Unanswered questions swirled between them, but they both kept to themselves, staring out across the landscape. Eva broke her silence to ask Pieter to stop along the way. He nodded his head, seeming to understand.

"He must be all grown up by now."

"He's growing fast."

"Do you think he'll remember me?"

Pieter never hesitated.

"Of course he will, Eva. You're his mother."

"Thank you for petitioning the State Department on my behalf, Pieter. How can I ever repay you?"

"You are the wife of a dear friend. Please ..."

The two moved comfortably into the past, recounting funny stories of family gatherings, neighborhood disputes, politics and gossip; of weddings, birthdays and funerals. Both of them understood how these memories served to bind them, a people now cast like grains of sand across the earth; tiny, insignificant, meaningless things that gave life meaning.

"I've missed Shimon," he said.

"As have I," she whispered. "What word of Izabel? How did you find her?"

"Here we are," Pieter interrupted. "Look, Eva, he's waiting for you."

Eva saw two little heads bobbing up and down on a sofa in front of a bay window. Eva barely had time to climb out of the car when the front door flew open and two small children bounded across the yard.

Cars and trucks lined up along the driveways and streets, and people poured out of their houses to witness the reunion.

Eva looked at her son in amazement. He was smaller-boned than his sister; he had his grandmother's refined features, and her curly, blonde hair. He was perfect. She drank him up with her eyes as he ran toward her. David stopped short to study his toes in the grass.

"Are you my mommy?"

"I am."

She grunted with the effort of lifting him, for he was heavier than he seemed, and she smothered kisses over his beaming face. He wiped off her lipstick and shyly touched her hair.

"Did you remember my surprise?"

"Of course she did," Pieter interrupted.

Pieter produced a gleaming black die-cast metal train set, complete with red caboose, from beneath his overcoat. David shrieked in his mother's ear and wriggled to free himself from her grasp.

"There you are, young man."

Pieter swaggered for the crowd. The women moved in to welcome Eva, and crowded around her in a wave of laughter and smiles, when Eva suddenly turned around.

"Where is Izabel?"

The women studied their hands and Pieter cleared his throat.

"She couldn't be here today," he said. "I'll explain it all to you later. Let's not spoil the day."

"Look," Pieter said, "Here's Frank Hencz from the Beacon News."

Eva looked around in dismay.

"Where's my son?"

"Can I get a picture of you with your boy?"

Pieter snatched David from the train set and plopped him in his mother's arms. David whimpered and looked to his sister for help, but Magdalena had already been sent to the kitchen to serve drinks. The shifting of power had already begun.

"Here, give your brother juice, Magdalena."

Magda crept towards her brother and offered him a cup of cider from her trembling hands.

"Don't you spill it," hissed Pieter.

Magdalena stood there, her lips quivering, when Eva caught sight of her. Her heart broke for the child standing alone in a sea of people. She reached out to pull Magda to her, when Pieter shoved her aside. The flash bulb popped.

The news story was offset with a photograph of David struggling against his mother's embrace. Closer inspection revealed the object of the boy's desire: His sister, serving juice in Dixie cups, across the crowded room.

Twenty-six

Izabel lay in the hospital bed and scratched idly at old wounds left by leather wrist restraints. She listened to the footfall of pedestrians crunching along the private drive, the compaction of snow percussive beneath their feet. Each day, the early-morning silence was broken by the high-pitched staccato of laughter and the rhythm of polite conversation beneath the cold gray, carbon-steel bars.

Frozen branches heaved and split beneath the weight of melting snow, drawing Izabel's ear in the direction of the noise. The sound came from the great white oak outside her window. The tree was grandfather to many young saplings in the nearby woods; born of acorns buried deep by absent-minded red squirrels. It was a tree that possessed supernatural strength and power. There were some in the Rromani community who understood the whisperings of these leafy monoliths, who spoke in an ancient tongue known only by the things of this earth.

Some time ago, the trees dripped thin, clear droplets of sap from the tips of their branches, splattering sweet water across the muddy landscape. It was the spring surge, brought on by an early thaw. The faintest blush of pale green peeked out from tiny nubs on the trees.

Suddenly, a blizzard ripped across the Fox River Valley, scouring the land of its tender buds. When the sun finally released the earth from winter's icy grip, hundreds of early-migrating robins were found frozen in the melting snow drifts. Coyotes and red-tailed hawks feasted on the carrion released from the frozen fingers of the Fox River; the oldest and the weakest of the white-tail, raccoon and opossum, surrendering their flesh with great reluctance in order to sustain new life.

A day after the blizzard, a wave of excitement swept through the hospital's recreation room. Mildly curious, Izabel abandoned her journal entry to follow the crowd of patients that ran howling past her. She shuffled through the security doors in her slippers outside to a walkway leading to an elevated garden. She stopped short to stare down at a young Northern snowy owl lying frozen on a bare patch of ground beneath the spiny remains of a summer rose. The rose was the Old-European *R. Damascena Trigintipetala*, the Kazanlik rose, one of Izabel's favorites.

The creamy down of the owlet's coat had been torn away in patches, exposing the flesh beneath. Scarlet droplets were slowly draining into the hard earth. Izabel heard the shrieking of crows gathered along the periphery, black demons coming to feast on his memory. Izabel felt the tiny, white hairs rise up along the back of her arms and neck. It was a sign. She knew what she had to do. Her infant daughter's spirit was restless. She was alone, without family, without peace. If she could not soothe her daughter's anger, she would torment Magdalena, and Magdalena's children, and so on, for countless generations. Izabel knew she must return to Hungary, she must bury her infant daughter in the Rromani way, and she must bury her among her own kind.

Izabel backed away from the peaceful sleeping face of the owlet, moving intuitively towards a cedar park bench near the security doors. She dropped wearily onto the frozen bench and pulled a pack of cigarettes from her sweater. Her fingers trembled as she struck a match and held it to the tip. She inhaled deeply, and watched as a security guard scooped up the sightless bird, and dumped it unceremoniously in a trash bag. Iza's eyes welled at the sight of the formless lump in the bottom of the Hefty bag.

A old woman standing near Izabel commented, "It must have lost its way in the storm."

"Poor thing."

"He should bury it in the garden. It shouldn't be tossed out with the garbage."

"I agree."

"Hey! Why don't you give it a proper burial? You have a shovel there. Just take a few minutes and bury the little fellow."

"And let you nuts dig it up later?"

"Shut up."

"You're a poophead."

"Poophead! Poophead!"

"Alright. Go back to your rooms. The freak show is closed for the night. The security guard turned to grin at Izabel. "I'll tuck you in later."

Izabel pulled a mighty drag from her cigarette and flicked it against the man's pant leg.

He glared at her. "Pick it up."

"Pick it up! Pick it up," mimicked the mental patients.

"Shut up! Goddamn freaks…"

"Leave her alone. She's just a girl," the old woman said.

The guard sneered at Izabel malevolently; he knew he had the upper-hand. His eyes moved eagerly over her familiar body, his thighs trembling with anticipation. He wasn't stupid. He remained a respectful distance from Izabel. Someone might be watching from the administrative wing.

"I *said* pick it up, Missy."

Izabel cried out and broke for the door. He lunged at her and caught her tiny wrist in one greasy hand.

"Are you fucking *deaf*? I told you to…"

Suddenly, Izabel felt his lecherous hands jerk away from her. She flinched at the sound of metal on bone as a cast-iron doorstop cracked against the back of the guard's skull. Izabel fell backwards onto her tailbone and yelped in pain.

She looked up to see a two hundred and fifty pound schizophrenic place two meaty thumbs over the security guard's eye sockets. The guard's high-pitched screams did not stop the man from pressing down on his face, the veins in his muscular forearms bulging with the effort. He smiled down at the guard writhing beneath him, his face childlike and serene, when Iza heard the first sickening pop.

The crowd swarmed around them like bees. They bellowed and gibbered and bleated like sheep. Izabel scurried backwards on all fours like a crab, trying to reach the door, her eyes frozen to the spot where the two men fell. The crowd broke for a split-second, and permitted Izabel an unobstructed view of the blood gushing down the guard's purple cheeks. She slammed into the security door and reached up for the door handle when it swung open, cracking against the back of her skull. Lights swirled behind her eyes and everything went black.

Several days later, Iza awoke from the tranquilizer. When a nurse came into her room to offer her tea, Izabel turned her face to the wall. Day after day, a parade of nurses, doctors and administrators stopped by to check on her. The doctors each looked at a section of her anatomy—pupils, reflexes, heart, lungs, bowels—disseminating her in parts, recording their observations, before moving on to the next set of parts.

The nurses were kind. They spoke to her as they moved about the room. They changed her bed sheets and exercised her limbs. After several weeks of Iza's catatonia, two nurses came into her room to hold her upright while a third fastened a sheet about her neck with a safety pin. The youngest nurse wept as Iza's unkempt hair was shorn to black stubble. Izabel lay limply in her arms without uttering a sound.

The fat nurse looked sadly at the young girl. "For shame," she mumbled.

The young priest from St. Nicholas Church prayed over Izabel as he fastened a pin of St. Jude, the Patron Saint of Lost Causes, around her neck. But God was with Iza now.

For as the mind-numbing routine of bed checks carried on, God, in His perfect wisdom and mercy, sent Izabel home again, running through expansive woodlands and the *Nagy-Alföld*, the great central plain of Hungary, playing hide-and-seek with her big brother, George.

George was Izabel's best friend when she was little—George with the blue-green eyes and black curls cascading down his back. George was mama's favorite child, for he reminded her of some relative long-since buried.

George was spoiled and lazy. He had the imagination of a god and the mind of a poet. He was a fantastic liar, weaving tales of spirits and faeries and sprites as they languished in the tall grasses by some unknown river's edge.

George was the boy who saw their father's glazed expression when the bottle was half-empty, who yanked his little sister half asleep from their tent to run beneath the stars, to wonder at the trees lit by the new moon.

George was the imp who whispered to Izabel that the cooing of a Turkish dove was actually the crying of a river nymph. He picked up leaves curled around spider silk, presenting them to her as the downy nests of woodland faeries. His eyes saw the tiniest details. He studied the variegations of the leaves and the seed-heads of the grasses.

He watched ants stealing insect larvae, he smelled rain on the wind, and he cried out to the trees that trembled at the prospect. The spirits of the air, the earth and water watched them, smiling, as the children tried to catch them dancing in the moonlight, or dozing in the flowers in the midday sun.

George was that rare child who breathed magic into life. He knew no fear. Iza never knew she was poor. She never knew she was ignorant or disadvantaged. God had given her a precious gift. She was an explorer, a treasure-seeker, a mystical goddess. She was the luckiest child in the world.

In a last desperate attempt to save her spirit, God had sent Izabel's mind back in time to her days of exploration with the spirit of her long-dead brother. George no longer lay in the ground with worms crawling in him; he was there beside her, in a perpetual state of age ten, old enough to understand encroaching manhood, and young enough to vigorously resist it.

Sometimes, Iza caught the scent of her mother, or heard her singing softly to the babies late at night. She used to admire her mother's slender ankles when she raised her skirts to wash the laundry and also despaired at the dark circles beneath her mother's eyes. Izabel was ashamed of the thick, muscular hands that had wrung out countless diapers; ugly, thick, ashy hands with ragged nails. She loved her mother's hands—and she hated them. Comforting hands. Sustaining, capable, life-giving hands.

She heard George calling. He waved to her and hastened her to his latest discovery. She saw Magdalena in his eyes; in his smile that could light up a room. Magdalena was his likeness. She embodied his carefree spirit, and Izabel despaired they had never met, for consumption had taken George before his eleventh year.

Sometimes she had dreams of Jael. The dreams were hazy. They frightened Izabel. One recurrent dream was of Magdalena standing at the mouth of a brackish river.

Magda carried her baby sister Jael in her arms, singing her a Rromani lullaby, as the river lapped gently at her feet. Magda gently laid the infant on the ground and wandered off into the nearby trees. First, the waves lapped at Jael's blue swaddling cloth, then the water soaked through and began to move her to and fro with the tide, then a giant swell rose, lifting her off the ground.

At the exact moment she became buoyant, Jael's green eyes seemed to lock on Izabel, until slowly the water came up to her chin, then her mouth, then her nose. One gurgling cry, a shudder, and she was rolling underwater, pulled down in the undertow, and then she was gone, swept out to the sea.

Izabel watched in horror as her baby bobbed up and down in the swift current, rolling over and over, banged hard against a rock, and then sank. She lay frozen, unable to move, unable to cry out to her oldest daughter. She watched in horror as Magda dashed up and down the shoreline, and screamed for her sister—screaming, screaming, screaming—unaware of the water slowly rising again, lapping playfully at her dancing feet.

Iza sobbed and moaned in her sleep, not noticing the woman who rocked her gently in her arms. Her eyes flew open wide when she recognized the sound of the voice.

"I'm here now, Iza. Don't cry. I won't leave you again; you are coming home with me. I've arranged everything."

"Eva?"

"I can't believe you're alive. You did it, Izabel! You saved my son. I owe you my life. The young priest, Father Crossen, said he will help us. Think of it, Iza, we'll all be together again. It will be just like old times!"

"Eva! Eva! *Eva!*"

Izabel sobbed in her friend's arms. She was barely able to put her thoughts into words or for the words on her lips to form speech. "What day is today?"

"It is Sunday. I arrived here three weeks ago. I haven't left your side since I found you."

The two women rocked each other and wailed, and the nurses slowly came to investigate. The hospital staff hugged one another and clapped their hands and spoke of the miracle in Room 7G. Despite her doctor's admonishment, Iza was released to the care of Father Crossen, who had heard of her perilous journey across Eastern Europe to America. Father Crossen loved women with all his heart and admired these two more than most.

Days later, Izabel moved about the hospital room. She packed her new suitcase with the few items she possessed, her shaved head covered beneath a red silk scarf lovingly tied by Eva. She shuffled about like an old woman as she moved around the noisy children wrestling on the floor.

"Are you happy to come home, sister?

"Yes."

But Iza eyed her suitcase with dread, knowing her past would always be there. It lapped at her feet, and the ghosts of the dead whispered in her sleep. At least at the hospital, the rooms were never empty; you were never alone to face your demons for long. She was afraid. A mind-numbing fear swept through her like an icy wind, which chilled her flesh to the bone. Who would save her from herself?

She sat on the bed with a weary thud and Eva plopped down beside her. Eva scolded David for pulling his sister's hair. She grabbed Iza's bony fingers in her soft hand.

"I am so excited! I hope you are happy here with us. The children and I have been getting your room ready. Magdalena has worked especially hard. She has been so excited these past few days, she has hardly slept."

"I'm sure I'll be happy."

"You can sleep as much as you like. We have fresh, white linens on your bed and a beautiful, handmade quilt from your neighbor, Ruth. The women are very upset about that business with Pieter. He was wrong, Iza. He should be locked away. He is no friend to me."

"He's only a man."

"No matter. His behavior was despicable. And to think how he was a dear friend to Shimon and me! I will look after you now, sister. You've suffered for too long."

Iza started to cry. "Will anyone ever love me?"

"I love you, mommy," whispered Magda.

The little girl crept over to her mother and rested her head in Izabel's lap. Iza recoiled from her daughter. She glared down at her with a ferocity that frightened Eva.

"Not now, Magdalena, your mother is tired."

Iza bent down to whisper in her daughter's ear. Eva leaned forward, but the words she heard were Rromani. Eva scolded herself for never learning the language.

"How can you say you love me?"

"I do love you, mommy."

"My heart is shattered, Magdalena. I am cursed to walk the earth alone. I have made a difficult choice. My heart has been burdened by the news of the child stolen from Eva at Auschwitz. Do you understand?"

The girl shook her head no.

"Eva's baby was taken from her womb before its first breath. Its spirit was lost forever. You have your father's loving heart. I will leave his heart with the one to whom it belongs. You are Eva's daughter now. You will take the place of the daughter she lost. Do you understand?"

The girl nodded.

"God willing, you will forgive me for sending your sister away. You will have a home here, Madgalena. Most importantly, you will be loved."

Magda went to Eva with tears in her eyes.

"Don't fret, Magda. Your mother is just tired."

When Iza stood up from her bed and closed her suitcase, the latch clicked shut with chilling finality. As Eva and Magdalena held each other on the bed with happy smiles, the two women and the little girl knew in their hearts that nothing would ever be the same again. The devil had come to collect his due.

And as Izabel plotted her escape from her only daughter's life, Magda seemed to have secret knowledge of her mother's sin. For on that day, the little Rromani girl disappeared inside herself for the last time, seeking only her brother David for comfort.

Twenty-seven

In the quiet moments before dawn, before the children rubbed their eyes and lurched into the kitchen to whine for breakfast, Izabel and Eva worked quickly. The wallop of bread dough against the butcher block table intermittently broke the comfortable silence. Next to the coffee percolator sat a thin package.

When Izabel untied the string and peeled back the paper, she found a writing journal adorned in red leather, with a tiny gold lock to keep the words safe from prying eyes. On the front cover, Izabel's name was skillfully embossed into the soft leather in brilliant gold script. Her bottom lip quivered as she opened the front cover and read aloud.

"To my beloved sister."

Izabel clutched the gift tightly to her chest and, once the oven swallowed the last bread pan, she disappeared to pen her first entry. Eva smiled to herself, pleased by her friend's reaction, for the doctors said she needed a creative outlet.

Long after the children went to bed, Eva and Izabel stayed up late. They drank wine and told stories about the people they loved. Eva told her about the brutal rape of twelve-year-old Rachel, about the shooting of elderly Jews on the march to Szeged, and about little Katarina, whom her embittered mother came to love in the days before her death. She told Izabel about how Sarai sacrificed her life to comfort the terrified Rromani child and, when she was finished, Eva laid her head on Izabel's knee and cried herself to sleep.

Eva was grateful for the rare peace, for she wondered sometimes if Izabel's mind were slipping. Since she arrived home from Mercy Hospital, Iza refused to groom herself or wash her soiled garments. She screamed at Magdalena from inside the front door if she caught her speaking to a boy, and smacked her daughter hard as she ran for the safety of the bathroom. She argued vehemently that a Rromani girl had no use for the sort of education that American public schools would provide.

"I will teach my child all she needs to know. What can they show her but how to be a second-class citizen? She is a Rromni."

"This is America, Izabel, *all* are created equal."

Izabel glared at her.

"And what about the women? Where do they fall in the pecking order? America is no different than Hungary, Eva."

Eva did not respond.

"Why do they stare?"

"They are staring because you're so beautiful."

Her laughter made Eva's skin crawl. "I am nothing."

"You come from a proud race. You are mother to Magdalena. And you are my dearest sister."

Izabel fell silent.

"This is the Promised Land, Iza. Your daughter's future is here, a future free from shame and persecution. She will be well-educated; she will make you proud. You've always been a survivor. Don't give up on us now."

Though Eva spoke angrily, Izabel had no response. She seemed haunted by something, something that chilled the blood in Eva's veins, something she was afraid to whisper, even in the darkness. Iza had the smell of death on her. Eva felt it when she passed Izabel's room in the hall, or saw her reflection in a mirror. Izabel was not the vibrant girl she once loved in Mártély. She had metamorphosed into a freak, deformed and ugly, mutated by her unforgiving environment.

As time passed, Iza did not rise early to help prepare bread in the early-morning darkness. She slept late, not leaving her room until midday. Eva struggled to work and care for the house and, soon, her sadness was replaced by irritation, bone-crushing fatigue, and despair.

Izabel grew silent. She watched the whirl of activity from her corner chair, her eyes moving warily about the room, observing the children or writing in her journal, while Eva took care of the immediate needs of the household. Iza gradually stole away for longer periods of time, leaving her daughter to her own devices.

Eva sensed a weaning-away between Izabel and her daughter. Magdalena's words were met with indifference, and the child soon turned to the only other adult in the house for comfort. The comforting was short-lived, for

Magda, caught in the crossfire, became an easy target for Eva's growing frustration.

Eva soon noticed the children ignoring Izabel, moving around her like an inanimate object to be avoided, or else risk a sound beating. But when Magdalena lay next to her mother, moving closer to feel her warmth, she gazed up at her mother's face. Eva, too, marveled at her peaceful sleeping face, how her wrinkles were plumped and smooth; how the early sunlight filtered through the blinds, catching the red highlights in her dark hair. Izabel appeared young and beautiful again.

Then, as soon as she awoke, the walls slammed up again, and the family moved around Izabel like a homebound cripple, loving her with the secret hope she would die soundlessly in her sleep, a burden to the living no more.

So, like an answer to a prayer, she slipped silently into the darkness, without a word or a whimper, leaving only a note on her daughter's pillow.

You will be loved.

Magdalena read the words over and over, then folded up the paper and placed it inside her dresser drawer, nestled among her rock collection and overdue library books. She decided not to tell Eva about the note. She wanted it secret, kept safe in her own heart.

For days Eva was beside herself with worry, until a neighbor called to say she saw Izabel sipping tea in Pieter's garden, in her nightdress, no less. Eva swore in outrage.

"That ungrateful bitch. She always was..."

She cut her words short as she saw Magdalena cowering inside the doorway. The little girl ran to her room and yanked open her dresser drawer, weeping bitterly as she tore her mother's note into tiny pieces, scattering them across the floor.

"I wish she was dead!"

Eva came up behind the hysterical child and put a hand on her head. Magdalena threw herself against Eva's legs.

"I'm sorry, child. I was wrong to say that. I love your mother."

"I hate her!"

"You are my daughter now. I will care for you as your mother cared for David in Hungary. Your mother cannot help what she does. Her heart is broken."

"I don't care. I still hate her."

"I will not speak her name again."

Eva left the girl sobbing on her bed and did something she'd never done before. She sat in her living room in the middle of the day, and drank wine and smoked the cigarettes Iza left behind.

Eva drank to her family, she drank to her husband, she drank to her parents, and she drank to the dead that haunted her dreams. She drank to their memory and cursed them for leaving her alone.

Can I love this child? How can I look on her without seeing Shimon's betrayal?

Sad little Magdalena, in her profound innocence, lay like an inconvenient burden Eva's heart just couldn't bear. She was a living testimony of God's injustice. Of the disgusting, random joke that had become her life.

I will not raise my husband's bastard!

Eva felt hatred burning in her heart for Magdalena, for all that she was, and was not, and in a moment of drunken fury, Eva rose to her feet and stumbled to the girl's bedroom to tear out her hair.

When she threw open the door, she found David curled in his sister's tight embrace, sucking his thumb noisily as he slept. Eva stood breathless, gazing at her children for many minutes, until she turned away, closing the door behind her.

Eva ran outside. When she was engulfed in darkness, she began searching the night sky for familiar points of light, and when she found the evening star of her youth, Eva fell to her knees and began to pray.

Twenty-eight

Izabel did not give a damn about Pieter. When he tried to comfort her, Izabel lashed out at him, destroying everything in her sight. He was a patient man, he loved her in his own way, and though his guilt bound him to her, his affection clouded his judgment.

Izabel heard that when the INS officer from Chicago appeared on Eva's doorstep, she handed him an address, written on a slip of paper, and shut the door. The officer later told a neighbor that he felt a chill on his spine as he turned from her stoop, wondering what devilry had passed between the two women.

Probably some man.

Pieter railed at the sight of him.

"Son-of-a-bitch!"

Izabel stared at Pieter with the hint of a smile on her lips, and the old man beamed, exhilarated at the sight of it.

"This fine woman will soon be my wife."

"Izabel Remény is in violation of U.S. and International Law. When I return, she'd better be ready to go."

Pieter slammed the front door against the immigration officer's backside and rushed to the doorway of Izabel's room. She laughed in his face, froze him in his tracks, his pained expression inciting even more laughter.

"Get out," she ordered.

He grabbed her arm, leaving a purple welt.

"If you ever touch me again, I will cut your throat in your sleep, you ugly little man."

"What?"

She snorted loudly at his confusion; how well he played the victim! But there would be no mercy for him this day.

"Do you think I like it when you push your tongue into my mouth and grunt over me like an old hog? You sicken me."

She sniffed at the air like a dog.

"You even smell old. Like rotting flesh. Touch me again and I'll kill you."

He stared at her, his mouth unhinged, bewildered and awe-struck.

"They were right about you. You are crazy. You evil bitch! I want you gone. Get out of my house."

Izabel pulled a long, stainless steel blade from beneath the mattress.

"No Pieter, you get out. I'm not afraid of you. Do you see? I fear no man."

Izabel took the blade and pulled it along the underside of her left hand, slicing the meat to the bone. She reached up and stroked Pieter's face, leaving a warm, red glob dribbling down his chin.

"Kiss me now, you old buzzard. How do you like me now, Pieter?"

Pieter recoiled like he'd been shot. He shoved her to the floor.

His voice rose in a scream. "I'm calling the hospital. You'll be admitted. You'll never see your daughter again!"

Her whisper was an urgent hiss—a taunting and defiant provocation. "Go ahead. I dare you."

He bolted from the room and ran to the kitchen. He lifted the telephone receiver and dialed the operator. He turned and saw Izabel illuminated in the doorway with the dripping knife in her left hand. She smiled at him sweetly as she shut the door in his face.

"Operator."

The telephone receiver shook in Pieter's hands. "Hello?"

"This is the operator. Is anyone there?"

Pieter returned the handset to the wall. After many minutes passed, he went to the sofa and turned on the television. He did not sleep for three days.

~ * ~

Mrs. Hencz sighed deeply as Magdalena spilt bitter tears. "The entire community came unglued when Izabel returned to Pieter. Pieter kept the shades drawn tight, his home under siege for weeks. A man walking his dog claimed to see Izabel crying in her bedroom, completely naked from the waist down. The pastor's wife whispered of having sighted Izabel in the garden, singing strange songs, and talking to the dead.

Even the police chief reported Izabel wandering the street late at night, hiding behind trees and flower planters when cars passed by. His officers dragged her by her nightdress to the squad car. They shone flashlights in her face and scrutinized the contents of her handbag. Izzy screamed curses at them from her front porch, waving her fists as they pulled away in their squad cars, laughing all the way down the block."

"*Just another harmless coot.*"

"*I'll bet we find her frozen under a train trestle by February.*"

Mrs. Hencz's hand shook slightly. "The neighborhood children tossed eggs at the house and wrote obscenities on the garage door. Izabel retaliated by layering a thick blanket of broken glass on top of her wooden fence. When boys gathered along the periphery of the yard, conspiring to smash windows or set a fire, Pieter rushed out onto the porch, sending them running."

"*Crazy Izzy! Crazy Izzy! Crazy Izzy!*"

The old woman's face burned with shame. "The good people of Aurora went off to work each day to provide for their families. They attended their churches and temples, worshipping the Lord and asking for His blessings. They donated food to the needy and collected clothes for the destitute. And they smiled secretly to themselves at the wicked girl's unraveling, hoping she would disappear altogether from their neat, orderly lives."

"*Stay away from her, boy. There's something wrong with that woman.*"

She paused for a moment to clear her throat. "When the immigration officer returned to Pigeon Hill a month later,

Izabel Remény was long gone. Rumors of foul play began to circulate. Suspicion surrounded Pieter for many months, until a hand-written letter arrived from Bulgaria, addressed to Eva.

The mailman, who carried the letter ceremoniously to Eva's front door, shuffled his feet in hopes she would read it aloud. Once interest in Izabel waned, Pieter's neighbors quietly returned to his side and, the terrible splinter finally removed, the community began the long, slow process of healing."

Mrs. Hencz's eyes filled with tears. "Everyone secretly thanked God for Izabel's departure, praying she would never return and disrupt their quiet lives again. Everyone except Eva. For only she knew Izabel's rage, bitterness and grief. Only she knew her friend's fear of intimacy, her fundamental mistrust, born of years of systematic abuse. Only Eva understood Izabel's childlike need for love and acceptance."

Mrs. Hencz wrapped her bony arms around herself and rocked back and forth in her chair. After a long moment of silence, the old woman fixated on Magdalena. "Love and acceptance. Two things Izabel never found, would never find. The Gypsy whore, the rare beauty, the mother, sister, the woman. Others breathed a collective sigh of relief, but Eva never fully recovered, for she had lost her sister for the second time in her life. And when Eva died many years later, it was from an irreversible hardening of her heart."

~ * ~

As Izabel's bus moved beyond city limits, she felt a joy she had not felt in years. She had survived and she would never look back. She would not compromise herself again. She would return home and bury the ghosts of her past, forever.

Twenty-nine

They raced down the road in their Avis rental, David still fuming over his tantrum at Budapest's *Ferihegy* airport.

"*I'm sorry, sir, we don't have any mid-sized vehicles. But we do have a wide selection of compact cars.*"

"*Do I look like I want to squeeze my 200-pound ass into a compact car, lady? Look, I reserved a mid-sized vehicle three months ago. So, explain to me, again, why there isn't one here.*"

The argument raged on for a half hour before Magdalena finally wandered out of the *Malév* Airline terminal and into the baggage-claim area.

What a perfect place for people-watching!

She saw a boisterous group of college students smoking cigarettes and playing grab-ass while they waited for their backpacks to appear on the carousel. Magda watched one long-haired boy, dressed in torn blue jeans and a concert tee, as he felt up his girlfriend by the public payphones.

In front of God, Country and Corps, as David would say.

She saw businessmen in dark suits briskly passing through, wheeling their luggage along behind them. Old women shuffled about in brightly colored blouses and long, flowing skirts. These were timeless women, thick and matronly, babushkas framing their wrinkled brows.

Magdalena loved the rich diaspora of humanity that could be found at international airports. She stared openly at passersby until an old woman glared at her menacingly. She muttered to herself as she passed, which prompted Magda to high-tail it back to the service counter.

"Let's go," David barked.

He grabbed their bags and headed towards the vehicle-staging area, storming a few feet ahead of her. The suitcases scraped along the ground, flipping sideways in gravelly patches with a thud, righting themselves again with a grunt.

As they drove towards the center of the great Eastern jewel, Magda was glad that it wasn't dark. The airport was a generous fifteen miles southeast of the city center, enough distance for her senses to be assailed by the sights and sounds of Budapest.

The city was a strange amalgam of old and new. Sprawling, large-scale industrial complexes pimpled the banks of the Danube. By the stench drifting downwind, it seemed obvious they lacked proper purification, and opted instead to dump directly into the river.

"Hungarian forests are being decimated by acid rain," David told her. "Bauxite, used to produce aluminum, is mined nearby, and aluminum rolling-mills dot the waterway. There is an iron and steel industry. Chemical plants supply pharmaceutical products and nitrogen fertilizer is produced from coal. Artificial fibers, rubber, paper and cellulose—all are manufactured here. There is even a processed-meat industry."

As David droned on about urban decay and Hungary's shift to a market economy, Magdalena only saw how the past flirted with the promise of Budapest. She saw scattered outposts of steel framework and fresh coats of paint, vestigial remnants of rebuilding and reconstruction: the Elisabeth Bridge, the old city centre, the castle quarter, and luxurious hotels on the Pest bank.

The phoenix that rose from the ashes.

Magdalena saw Budapest through gentler eyes, and felt an instant kinship to her people, for the city was like an early spring flower that bloomed from beneath the snow. Its history was marked by struggle without hope, against tyrants and invaders. Though subjugated time and again, the people still rose vigorously against their oppressors.

Her heart leapt at the thought. Not wishing to torment the raging tiger, she let David rant. He would cool down and listen, in time.

Izabel lived in a fringe district, an outer domicile of the working-class. The grandeur of castles and cathedrals was soon replaced by dull, high-rise apartment flats in trash-strewn neighborhoods. Upon spying Izabel's address, David tore around the block to find parking. Butterflies danced in the pit of Magda's stomach. She felt bile rising in her throat.

"I think I'm going to be sick."

"No, you're not," David said, matter-of-factly, "Relax, sister. I'm right here beside you; I'm not going anywhere."

He squeezed her trembling hand, smiling at her reassuringly. "Let's do this!" He jumped out of the car and raced to the curb.

Just breathe.

"You okay?"

I'm not crippled, you know!

"I'm fine."

They swung open heavy glass doors and stepped inside a dimly-lit foyer. David searched the mailboxes along the wall.

"Yep. Here she is."

Suddenly, a buzzer sounded shrilly overhead. Magda swung around to face the noise, nearly knocking David off his feet. They both laughed, the tension broken.

"Ready?"

"Ready as I'll ever be."

They entered the elevator and David pressed the button. The elevator shuddered and creaked on rusty chains, eventually depositing them on the seventh floor. When Magda stepped out of the elevator, something drew her attention; an odd movement in her periphery. A young girl waved at her from an apartment to her left.

"Dordi, dordi! Púridaia! Av akai!" She squealed with excitement, waving her hands over her head, as she jumped up and down in the doorway. She shouted something in rapid-fire Hungarian and people began pouring out into the hallway. Most of the children were screaming and clapping their hands, while the grown-ups wept and covered their faces.

The crowd approached and gathered her to them. Everyone took turns hugging and kissing her, and those standing close touched her hair and squeezed her hands. She was overcome by joy, and by grief. The group engulfed her in their midst and retreated back inside the apartment. She turned to find David.

Which one is Izabel?

Then she recognized the old woman sitting in a wheelchair beside the radiator, the sun beaming down on her smiling face.

"Mama?"

"Come here, daughter. Let me see your face."

Magda stood in front of her.

"I can't see you."

Magda leaned down to kiss her cheek and the old woman reached out to touch her.

One man volunteered, "Your mother has been blind for many years now."

Izabel stroked her daughter's hair and touched her wet face. Tears streamed out of her sightless eyes.

"You are so beautiful to me. Is she beautiful, Jael?"

Magdalena gasped, shocked at the sight of the young woman who crept silently from the kitchen, a wooden spoon in one hand.

"Welcome, sister. I am happy to meet you."

The girl moved to her mother's side. When Magdalena held out her hand, the slender girl smiled and embraced her, kissing her on the mouth.

"She has Rromani hair, mother. Yes, she is beautiful."

The room fell silent as the family waited for Magda's reaction. She was speechless. The girl was the mirror-image of her mother in her youth.

"Are you alright, sis'?"

David touched her shoulder.

"I remember now. I thought she was gone," Magda whispered.

"She was alive," said her mother, "and she was right where we left her. For many years, I had lost faith, but God delivered her in His time. Do you remember the promise I made to you, daughter?"

The old woman clasped her hands to her mouth.

"As I swore to your father, so it has finally come to pass. Your brother has brought you home. Thanks to God!"

Magda clung to David.

Izabel asked, "Please, leave us alone."

"What is that tantalizing aroma?" asked David.

"Come and see," the women cried.

The young girls giggled and pulled him along to the kitchen. Magda could hear the women proudly offering first taste.

"This is *Halászlé*. It's a soup of fish, onions and vegetables, spiced with hot paprika and sour cream."

"Here is some milk bread."

"Try my strudel filled with apples, some with cherries, and nuts, poppy seeds and curd cheese."

"Do you want apricot brandy, beer or coffee?"

~ * ~

The sisters stood facing one another. The room was uncomfortably silent.

Izabel broke the tension. "Her hair is dry," she said. "She has not been shown how to care for it. Show her, Jael."

"Wait! I'll get the oil."

Magdalena's face burned with embarrassment. "N-no, thank you. I should find my brother."

Jael clicked her tongue sassily at her sister.

"He looks like he's doing just fine to me." She pushed Magdalena onto a worn upholstered chair and brushed her hair to a high shine. Then she pulled a small amount of warm oil through the dry, brittle strands.

"You used to sing to me when I was a baby. You used to rock me and sing to me when I cried."

Magda choked at the memory. "Yes."

"Mama has told me much about you. You were a very brave little girl. Strong and brave. You were my guardian angel. And now I will be yours."

~ * ~

Six months after their reunion, Izabel finally returned to the spirit world. Her passing was peaceful, for she knew she had been forgiven. And as she breathed her last, her beloved daughters lay beside her, defying Rromani custom in their profound grief.

"I will be glad to see Eva again," she whispered to Magda, "I've missed her so."

So passed another sinner, a fallen woman, into an eternal state of grace. Not redeemed by her birthright, or by privilege or wealth, but by her courage, her spirit, her passion, and her innocence.

The next day, the sisters found an old, forgotten journal stuffed inside a dresser drawer. Magdalena had been wrong. She *was* loved. She *was* cherished.

Choices made in the span of a lifetime can ripple outward for generations; every action, every word, triggering events beyond our control. A tiny pebble dropped into a reflecting pool moves the water outward and then back again; shifting ripples into waves.

Magda wondered how the decision of one man to follow his heart could create such a storm, piercing so many lives with its percussive roar. The pool was calm now, but soon her time would come, and she would drop her pebble down. She was free to face the world without shame. She was free to live, and love freely, for she knew she was loved.

Thirty

Droplets of rain clung deep inside the shivering husks that withered, papery and prostrate, in the baking summer heat. The fiery dragon moved fast across the prairie flats, breathing out its scorching breath, a hint of rain in the taste of it.

The farmer sat inside his drafty kitchen watching the raindrops hug the branches of the old cottonwood his grandfather planted as a boy. Though he had many chores yet to do, he watched the green-eyed girl playing with her dog beside a shimmering field of corn.

The dog shook the rain off his bedraggled coat, spraying water across her favorite flowered dress.

"Bad dog," she scolded.

His ears lifted in surprise. His tail wagged as he smiled up at her. She spun around in a circle, her dress lifting high in the air. She twirled on her toes, laughing, and the dog bounded away, turning back to bark at her.

She pulled the long, black curls away from her face and peered down into the rushing creek. She picked up a stick to poke at the tadpoles and crawfish clinging desperately to rocks and tree roots. She dislodged them, laughing when they tumbled end-over-end in the current.

The farmer rose to call out the window. "Stay away from the water!"

"Someone's here, Nikolai," his wife called. "Can you get the door?"

Annoyed at being disturbed, he said, "I can't now. Tractor's still down."

His wife sighed heavily as she pulled open the door. "Yes?"

Silence.

"Can I help you?"

Still silence.

"Nikolai. Come here, please."

The farmer froze at the sight of the bedraggled woman standing on his doorstep. She was still relatively young, though faded. Her green eyes shone bright above black circles. The woman reached out to touch his wife's hand.

"Please, madam. I've come a long way to find her."

His wife bristled. "Who?"

The Rromani woman sighed deeply. "My daughter."

His wife stuttered, "I don't know what you're talking about, Madame. You're not welcome here. Please leave this house."

"Please, listen to me."

"No. I won't. Please go. *Nikolai!*"

"I left my baby here many years ago. I left her inside that barn at the back of your property. Please tell me where she was buried."

"Nikolai!"

Nikolai moved from the kitchen doorway. "What do you mean?"

"Her spirit left me that night. Where did you bury my baby?"

"Oh, you are mistaken, Madame."

"No, Nikolai" cried his wife.

"There *was* a baby left inside of our barn by a young woman. Many years ago ..."

"*Get out of my house!*" His wife shoved against the door with both hands.

"I'm sorry?" Izabel pushed back against the door.

"Please, wife!"

"For God's sake, Nikolai. She's a Gypsy. She abandoned her; left her for dead. You heard it from her own lips."

He grabbed her wrist to pull her into his arms. "She's not ours." Then, more gently, "She's not ours."

His wife broke free from his grasp and thundered up the stairs. She slammed the bedroom door. The walls reverberated, then all was silent. Nikolai looked at Izabel, trembling on his doorway.

"Why did you run away when I called you? We could have helped you."

"You know why."

He stared hard at her for many minutes.

"Come with me."

He glanced upstairs where his wife lay crying for the children God wouldn't allow her. He held the screen door for Izabel and they walked into the backyard.

Izabel froze in her tracks when she saw Jael spinning on her toes while her dog barked madly at her flying skirts.

"My God," she cried.

The old man waved the girl over.

"Yes, Papa?"

"This is your mother," he said. The farmer turned and walked away.

Izabel fell to her knees and gathered Jael into her lap. The dog growled menacingly at the strange woman until Jael silenced him. The little girl gazed upon her mother's face for several minute and then she smiled.

"It's alright," said Jael, "don't cry. He can't hurt you anymore."

Izabel did cry. She cried for the living and the dead. She cried for her lost innocence and she cried for second chances. She praised God for delivering her daughter, and she felt her spirit begin to heal. She spilled an ocean of tears that day, tears of fury and tears of joy. She was free to travel the path of her choosing along a wide and pleasant road.

We are each a single thread in His loom. The Weaver's hands fly and his right foot taps on the treadle. Back and forth, the wooden shuttle flies from right hand to left and back again, between the even threads of warp. Swiftly, the threads of warp crisscross each other, catching fast the thread the shuttle leaves behind.

And the tapestry stretches out for generations. The pattern appears random when seen up close, but divine understanding brings about order and beauty in its perfection.

"*I will write in my journal each day, Magdalena, I will keep alive the news of Jael. We will be waiting for you, daughter. I will find the courage to meet each day anew. I will work hard. I will not forget you.*"

Meet

P. L. Reid

Pamela Reid lives, works and writes in a house surrounded by woods outside a small farming community in LaSalle County, Illinois. P.L. Reid has worked as a freelance editor and writer for twenty-five years, most-recently as Managing Editor for *Arts Beat Magazine*. In September 2005, Reid was awarded a scholarship by Tony-nominated playwright, screen writer, actor and producer Samm Art Williams. P.L. Reid was also an assistant editor at *MidWeek Magazine* in Kaneohe, Hawaii and wrote a weekly column for Channel 2 in Honolulu. Her poems and short stories have appeared in *Arts Beat* and *Connections* literary art magazines. Reid was recently a featured artist at the "Art Around the Fox" fine arts festival in recognition of her published work.

*VISIT OUR WEBSITE
FOR THE FULL INVENTORY
OF QUALITY BOOKS*:

http://www.wings-press.com

*Quality trade paperbacks and downloads
in multiple formats,
in genres ranging from light romantic
comedy to general fiction and horror.
Wings has something
for every reader's taste.
Visit the website, then bookmark it.
We add new titles each month!*